MW01634393

Aliens on the Moon

ALIENS
ON THE MOON

A NOVEL ... OF SORTS

THOMAS KING

HarperCollins*Publishers*Ltd

Aliens on the Moon
Copyright © 2025 by Dead Dog Café Productions Inc.
All rights reserved.

Published by HarperCollins Publishers Ltd

FIRST EDITION

HarperCollins books may be purchased for educational, business, or
sales promotional use through our Special Markets Department.

HarperCollins Publishers Ltd
Bay Adelaide Centre, East Tower
22 Adelaide Street West, 41st Floor
Toronto, Ontario, Canada
M5H 4E3

www.harpercollins.ca

HarperCollins Publishers
Macken House, 39/40 Mayor Street Upper
Dublin 1, D01 C9W8, Ireland
https://www.harpercollins.com

Library and Archives Canada Cataloguing in Publication

Title: Aliens on the moon : a novel...of sorts / Thomas King.
Names: King, Thomas, 1943- author.
Identifiers: Canadiana (print) 2025018754X | Canadiana (ebook) 20250187698
| ISBN 9781443475891 (hardcover) | ISBN 9781443475907 (ebook)
Subjects: LCGFT: Novels.
Classification: LCC PS8571.I5298 A79 2025 | DDC C813/.54—dc23

Printed and bound in the United States of America

25 26 27 28 29 LBC 5 4 3 2 1

*For Jan Souto and Murray Sinclair. The stories they told.
The stories they will always be.*

Aliens on the Moon

The Paranal Observatory in the Atacama Desert of northern Chile is the first to raise the alarm. In quick order, SALT in South Africa, Roque de los Muchachos on La Palma in the Canaries, Mauna Kea on Hawaii, and SPT in Antarctica all confirm the Paranal observation.

Aliens have landed on the moon.

Three days after the aliens arrive from deep space and park their ship on the moon, Nico Karras is at the local Subaru dealership, where the tow truck has brought his new Forester.

Gary Tidy is behind the service desk.

"This is the fourth time it's happened," Nico tells Gary. "I get in the car, and it won't start."

There's a television set in the service waiting area, and CBC News is looping an enlarged image of the moon.

Gary points to the television. "Did you know that all the places on the moon have Latin names?"

"My car?"

"The spaceship landed in Mare Imbrium."

The pictures on the television are grey and grainy, and Nico can't see much that resembles a spaceship.

"I think there's something wrong with the electrical system."

"'Mare Imbrium' means 'Sea of Rains.' Kinda cool."

"I'm concerned," says Nico, "that there could be a systemic flaw in the car that is draining the battery."

"Missed you last week," says Gary. "Chuck almost got an eagle on the eighth."

"Been busy," says Nico.

"How's your mum?"

"The battery?"

"She settling into Falling Leaves okay?"

"Autumn Leaves. The battery?"

Gary looks away from the television to his monitor. "We'll give it a quick charge and see how that works."

"And if that doesn't fix the problem?"

"Then it could be a bad battery."

"Which Subaru will replace?"

"Can you believe it?" Gary hums the opening bars from *Star Wars*. "There actually is intelligent life in the universe."

When Nico gets back to the house, Sudi is sitting on the sofa, watching the continuing coverage of the aliens on the moon.

"You're just in time," she tells Nico. "They're expecting the aliens to exit their ship any moment now."

"*They* being?"

"See those guys?" Sudi waggles a finger at two men in suits who are having an animated conversation. "They're experts."

"On what?"

"And your mother called." Sudi twirls a finger in the air.

"Let me guess." Nico sits down on the sofa with a thud. "Autumn Leaves is a dump? She wants to move back to her old house? Should have had a daughter? Have I missed anything?"

"You'll never make her happy. She's angry because she's lost control of her life."

Nico stares straight ahead at the television. "Why is the sound off?"

"Have you ever listened to experts?"

Nico gets a glass of water from a push spout on the refrigerator door. It's a feature of the appliance that he likes. The water is cold, so you don't have to rummage in the freezer for ice cubes.

"Autumn Leaves is a great place," says Nico. "It sure as hell isn't cheap."

"I think we can assume that the aliens didn't come all this way just to sit on the moon." Sudi turns away from the screen. "How's your car?"

"They charged the battery."

"Didn't they do that last time?"

THE NEXT MORNING, THE car won't start. The guy who arrives is the same guy who towed the car the day before.

"Didn't we tow you yesterday?" The patch on the guy's coveralls says HECTOR.

"We did."

"And now the car won't start? Again?"

"It might not be the battery," says Nico. "There could be something wrong with the car itself."

Hector opens the hood. "Hey, you interested in snow removal?"

"Now?"

"Course not," says Hector. "In the winter. Gary just got a pickup with a snowplow. He's signing people up. Now's the time to get on the list."

"I normally do it myself," says Nico.

"Number one cause of heart attacks." Hector hands Nico a card that says TIDY PROPERTY MANAGEMENT. "Bet he'd give you a good rate. Seeing as you guys play golf together."

"Right now," says Nico, "number one priority is the car."

"You have to wonder." Hector hooks the Subaru up to the tow truck. "Aliens land on the moon, and now your car doesn't work."

GARY IS WAITING FOR him when Nico arrives at the service desk. There's a woman standing next to him.

"I have good news."

"Good news is always appreciated," says Nico.

"This is Brenda Price," says Gary. "She's the assistant sales manager. I'll let her explain."

Brenda Price is a handsome woman with an electric smile that Nico associates with politicians and cheerleaders.

"We're going to get you a new battery."

"And will that solve the problem?"

"Evidently, the battery that came with the car isn't strong enough to keep up with all the electronic features."

"So, is Subaru going to issue a recall notice?"

"Not at this time," says Brenda. "Our recommendation is that you drive the car more to keep the charge up."

"If it sits too long without running," says Gary, "the problem could return."

A murmur goes up from the lounge area. Nico turns to see customers and some of the sales staff staring at the television.

"The door opened this morning," says Brenda. "It's pretty exciting."

"The door?"

"On the spaceship."

"And then the door closed," says Gary. "And you know what that means."

"So, you're saying that if I don't drive my car for a certain number of kilometres each and every day, the battery will go flat?"

"It means that the aliens are out," says Brenda.

"You know how crazy that sounds?"

"You don't just open and close a door for the hell of it," says Gary.

"No, I mean, what if I want to go on a camping trip? That's

what Subaru advertises, isn't it? Take your Forester into the woods. It can handle the great outdoors. Put up a tent by the lake. Do some fishing. Stay for two or three days. Get back in your car and drive home."

"It's a bit creepy," says Gary, "because now we have no idea where they are."

"Except in this case, when I get back in my car, in the middle of nowhere, it may not start."

Brenda smiles her "push 'em back, push 'em back harder" smile. "Subaru's very good about fixing stuff like this."

"And in the meantime?"

"I'd hold off on the camping trip."

The immediate problem, Gary explains, is that the dealership doesn't have a replacement battery in stock.

"The car is a new model, and so is the battery. We've looked around, but we can't find a single battery in North America."

"You're kidding."

"I wish I were," says Gary. "But we're getting one in from head office."

"Which is where?"

"Tokyo," says Gary. "Always wanted to go there."

Nico looks at Brenda. Then he looks at the cars on the showroom floor. "Is that a Forester?"

"Yes, it is."

"Same model as mine?"

"Except for the colour."

"And how long is it going to be before I get another battery?"

"I see where you're going with this," says Brenda, "but we can't swap batteries."

"Why not?"

"Company policy," says Brenda. "Do you have our extended warranty?"

There are several loud gasps. Nico turns to see a banner headline flash across the television that reads THEY'RE HERE!

"Started this morning," says Gary. "After the door opened, an astronomer in Hawaii spotted a smaller craft leaving the lunar surface."

Nico turns back to Brenda. "Does the extended warranty mean that you'll provide me with a rental?"

"It does."

"Then I'll take it."

"Problem is," says Brenda, "you have to buy the warranty at the time of purchase."

"So, I'm going to be without a car for what? A week, two? Because Subaru makes faulty batteries?"

"Look at that," says Gary. "They're projecting that the little ship is headed our way."

Sure enough, the diagram on the screen shows an arc from the moon to Canada.

"Be cool if they landed here." Gary looks up, as though he can see through the prefab metal ceiling of the showroom. "Put us in the history books."

"Maybe they'll have a battery for my car."

"Not a good idea," says Brenda. "Third-party parts could void the warranty."

THE DEALERSHIP SHUTTLE SERVICE takes Nico to the Enterprise office on Woodlawn.

"I need to rent a car."

"Compact, intermediate, or premium?"

"I have a Subaru Forester, so something like that."

"We have a Nissan Rogue or a Nissan Murano."

"No Subarus?"

The young man at the counter explains about the insurance waiver and the need to bring the car back with a full tank and how his credit card will be immediately credited for any damage to the vehicle.

"Would you be willing to fill out a customer-satisfaction survey?"

"Pass."

The young man has Nico initial the contract in eight places. "If you fill out the survey, you'll be eligible for an all-expenses-paid weekend in Ottawa."

By the time Nico gets home, the news on the television is all about a spacecraft that has landed in southern Alberta.

"Standoff," Sudi tells him. "Evidently, it's a Blackfoot reserve. The tribe has issued a press release saying that the ship is now under the protection of the sovereign Blackfoot nation. Evidently, they're not going to let anyone near it until Ottawa settles their land claim."

"Okay."

"Evidently, the Blackfoot were cheated out of land by the railroad, and now they want it back."

"Why would aliens land on an Indian reserve?"

Sudi mutes the TV. "I need to talk to you about something."

Nico waits.

"And I don't want you to start shouting."

Nico lets out a long sigh.

"No, it's not about your mother." Sudi shifts on the sofa. "It's Oceana."

Nico frowns, does a quick run through his mental Rolodex. "Who's Oceana?"

Sudi closes her eyes, shakes her head. "My sister?"

"You mean Evaline?"

"She changed her name. Remember?"

"I thought she changed it to Natalie."

"She did," says Sudi. "And then she changed it to Oceana."

Nico wants to say something clever, something snarky.

"You want to say something clever and snarky." Sudi crosses her arms on her chest.

"Don't tell me. She's getting married." Nico says this in his calm voice, the one he reserves for special moments such as this. "Again."

"This is why I don't tell you things."

"How many times does that make?"

"The issue," says Sudi, "isn't how many times my sister has been married."

So far as Nico can remember, Evaline-cum-Natalie-cum-Oceana has been married five times.

"Four times," says Sudi. "The one at the commune doesn't count."

"Remember her last bright idea? The destination wedding? Santorini? Bride and groom on donkeys? The Kalamatianos lessons?"

"And as you will recall," says Sudi, "that never happened."

"Because no one could afford to go."

"It would have been nice," says Sudi. "You could have gone back to Greece. The land of your forefathers."

"Santorini isn't Greece," says Nico. "It's an international tourist trap."

Sudi gives Nico an air kiss. "Your mother would certainly like to move back to Greece."

"Couldn't be any more expensive than Autumn Leaves."

"New Zealand," says Sudi. "This time Oceana wants to get married on a beach on the South Island."

"Why not get married on the moon?" says Nico. "That's closer."

At the end of the week, Nico drives to the dealership.

"No good news, I'm afraid," Gary tells him. "I think everything has slowed down because of the alien threat. You think they're serious about the manifesto?"

Nico tries to pretend he knows what Gary is talking about.

"In the meantime, we're playing Wednesday. You going to be able to make it?"

"Do you know how much it costs to rent a car?"

"Brenda really appreciates your patience," says Gary. "Some of our customers can be unreasonable."

Sudi is in the hammock, reading a book. Nico pulls up a chair, sits down next to her.

"Did you see the alien manifesto?" Sudi hands Nico her tablet. "It's all over the internet, and it's causing quite the stir."

The manifesto has a prologue and a list of three demands. Nico reads it once and then he reads it again.

"The aliens wrote this? In English?"

"I'm guessing it's a translation," says Sudi.

Nico enlarges the font on the tablet, so he can read without squinting. "Number one," he says. "All weapons of mass destruction are to be abolished? Okay, just how do they expect us to do that?"

Sudi shades her face with a hand. "Well, we did make them."

"Number two. We are to reduce our population to a planetary total of no more than two billion human beings."

"Easiest way to do that would be through birth control."

"Tell that to India and Africa."

Sudi looks at Nico. Nico looks at the clouds in the sky.

"Reduce emissions and limit consumption?"

"I read an article that said the U.S. is the worst offender," says Sudi. "And that Canada isn't far behind at number ten."

"I suppose they want us to go back to living in caves."

"That sounds like the battery talking."

ON THE WEEKEND, A cluster of world leaders arrive at the United Nations. The colours on the broadcast are off. The U.S. president looks slightly orange, while the president of Russia looks somewhat grey. Both men denounce the illegal landing on the moon by aliens and agree their manifesto is *ipso facto* a declaration of war.

Nico has to look up *ipso facto*.

"It's Latin," Sudi tells him.

"Why can't they just use English?"

"Do you think the U.S. and Russia are really going to attack the moon?"

"Without proper supervision," says Nico, "there's no telling what those two lug nuts will do."

"I don't imagine an assault would make the aliens too happy."

"Does the manifesto say what's going to happen if we don't comply with their demands?"

"Maybe they'll make the changes for us," says Sudi. "That would certainly be quicker than waiting."

ON FRIDAY, BRENDA PRICE calls to say that the battery for his Forester is in, but when Nico gets to the dealership, Gary has bad news.

"It's the wrong battery, Nico. The unit they sent is for the Outback."

"You know, it would make life easier if Subaru made one battery for all their cars."

"Standardization?"

"Exactly."

"Sharp edge of the wedge," says Gary. "You make a standard battery that fits all cars, and then you wind up making just one car, and that's the end of capitalism and democracy as we know it."

"So, now we have to start all over with the battery?"

"Small price to pay for our way of life. How's the rental working out?"

"It's a gas guzzler," says Nico. "And it's not particularly nimble."

Gary smiles. "Nothing like the Forester."

"At least the Murano starts when I press the button."

"Sure," says Gary, "but does it have EyeSight driver assist technology and a Harman Kardon sound system?"

On Saturday, a message on the internet goes viral.

"Not encouraging." Sudi pours cornbread batter into a cast-iron skillet. "But we might have expected something like this."

Nico checks the tablet. "If we don't reduce the birth rate, they're going to cull the human race?"

"It would help with global warming," says Sudi. "Remember that article in *Mother Jones*? The one about the effect the elimination of Native populations in North America had on the temperature of the planet?"

"Killing Indians lowered the temperature?"

"Most of the deaths were due to the diseases that Europeans brought with them, but the result was that all the lands the Indians had under cultivation were returned to their nature state. Consequently, between the late 1500s and the early 1600s, the new forests that were created soaked up enough carbon dioxide to lower the temperature by .15 centigrade."

"Do we even know if the aliens wrote this?"

Sudi puts the cast-iron skillet into the oven and sets the timer. "Of course, we could just do what they want us to do."

"Not a good idea."

"Why not? We've been talking about eliminating weapons of mass destruction for years. We know that we need to control the planet's population and reduce our emissions. We know that our level of consumption is insane. It's not as though any of this is new."

"It's a slippery slope," said Nico. "If we do what the aliens want, they'll just come back with more demands."

"Such as equal pay for equal work, and the end to racism?"

"Joke all you want," says Nico, "but if we let them push us around now, in fifty years, we won't recognize the place."

Two weeks later, Gary calls to say that the new battery is in. Nico takes the Nissan back to Enterprise.

"Can I get a ride to the Subaru dealership?"

"Absolutely," says the young woman at the counter. "How was the Murano?"

"Hard on gas," says Nico.

"My boyfriend says that the aliens are going to force us into electric cars."

"Maybe they'll make better batteries than Subaru."

"Would you be willing to fill out a customer-satisfaction survey?"

"No thanks."

"You could win a free rental for the weekend."

"What happened to the weekend in Ottawa?"

"That was last week," said the woman.

GARY AND BRENDA ARE waiting for him when he gets to the dealership. "Sorry it took so long," Brenda tells Nico. "Something such as this is an anomaly."

"Sort of like aliens on the moon."

"Exactly," says Brenda.

Gary takes Nico out to the parking lot and starts the car, so Nico can see that the battery is working.

"We think we discovered the problem." Gary opens up the back hatch. "You see this switch?"

Nico leans in so he can see what Gary is talking about.

"It has three positions. Off, on, and on when the door is open."

"What does it do?"

"In many of the cases where the battery has failed, we've discovered that the switch was in the on position." Gary toggles the switch back and forth. "We think it drains the battery, so we're suggesting that you leave it off unless you happen to need it."

"What does it do?"

"We also washed the car." Gary hands Nico a gift bag. "Brenda insisted that we give you a Subaru hat and a T-shirt to show you how much we appreciate your loyalty."

Nico adjusts the hat and puts it on.

"Very smart," says Gary.

The T-shirt is a large. Nico holds it up against his chest and debates whether he should trade it for the next size up.

Gary presses the auto close button on the hatchback. "If the aliens take over the government, you think they might have a look at our tax structure?"

SUDI IS SITTING IN front of the television, watching a special CBC News report. "You just missed an interview with the head of the

Centers for Disease Control. Want to guess how the aliens are going to handle the population problem?"

Nico gets a beer from the refrigerator. "Probably with a virus of some sort."

"That's certainly what happened to Indigenous populations in the Americas," says Sudi. "Smallpox, measles, influenza, tuberculosis. In the current situation, I guess you could argue for poetic justice."

"Not going to happen," says Nico. "Even the aliens wouldn't know what to do with a pile of five billion dead bodies. Talk about raising emissions."

"They wouldn't have to do it all at once," says Sudi. "They could space it out over ten, twenty years. Right now, there are about 132 million births each year and a little more than 55 million deaths."

Nico tries to do the math in his head.

"So, if you reduced the birth rate to, say, 20 million worldwide and kept the death rate at its current level, you'd lose an extra 35 million people each year. Add in a couple of minor pandemics that would kick the death rate up to 150 million per annum, and, in a little over thirty years, you would have reached your goal."

Nico tries to remember if a billion has nine zeros or twelve.

"From there on, it would just be a matter of maintenance."

Nico sits on the sofa and considers the dilemma. "If we kept our weapons of mass destruction," he says at last, "we could start World War III and accomplish the same thing in a shorter period of time."

"That's an awful idea," says Sudi, "but the logic is sound."

"All in all," says Nico, "I suppose we're not an easy species to understand."

"We do seem to work against our own best interests."

"I'm thinking about turning the Subaru in and getting an electric car."

"Is this the aliens talking?"

"It's more proactive than the prime minister's prayer vigil."

"What do you think the aliens are going to do?"

"Maybe they'll get bored and just leave."

"What about your mother and her wanting to move back to her house?"

"Not happening," says Nico. "Remember that fire?"

"Place hasn't sold yet," says Sudi, "so we still have the option."

That night, Nico can't sleep. He wanders around the living room, and then he goes to the backyard, stands in the dark, looks up. If aliens came all this way, why park on the moon? They could have landed in a desert or on a deserted island or gone down into the deep ocean where no one could see them.

He'll call his mother in the morning and explain once again why she can't live on her own, explain once again why a long-term care facility is the best of all worlds.

And then he'll go play golf with the rest of the guys.

Now that the battery problem has been settled.

Richard Dock lies in bed, not quite awake, not quite asleep, and sorts through the positive fragments of his life.

It doesn't take long. There aren't that many pieces.

He has his health. He has a house.

Well, *technically*, it's his sister's place. Darby owns it. And it's not a house. It's a condo. Richard—Dick to his family—would have preferred a bungalow on South Turner, but the sixth-floor, one-bedroom, one-bath at the Lagoon on Erie is almost as good. He's supposed to cover the property taxes, but they have proven to be a challenge, so Darby pays them as well.

Along with the utilities, the insurance, and the strata fees.

Not that Dick is satisfied with his life, not that he is content. Each morning, he sits on the balcony, waits for the Lucky Charms in his bowl to soak up the milk, and goes through an inventory of things he should have but doesn't.

A car. A cellphone. A rich girlfriend.

Okay, he can do without a car. Insurance, licence, maintenance, skyrocketing fuel prices. The downward spiral of depreciation.

At least he has a computer. It's a laptop. He'd like a desktop with two monitors, but the old Dell will have to do for the time being.

With it, he can upload his profile to MillionaireMatch, Date a Cougar, Ashley Madison, and join the waiting list for Raya.

And he'll do just that as soon as he fills out the necessary forms, answers the required questions.

Name?

Annual income?

Relationship status?

Tell us about yourself. Maximum of 2,000 words.

But there's a problem. This is personal information, and Dick isn't comfortable sharing his life with complete strangers. And he'd like to see some photos first. He'd like to see who might be available.

Look at the menu.

This seems reasonable. But if he doesn't have a cellphone, and he finds someone who looks interesting, how will he be able to call her? How will she be able to call him?

Sure, there's a landline in the condo, but how pathetic is that? It's not the twentieth century. He's explained all this to his sister on more than one occasion.

Then there are the things he doesn't have and doesn't want. A pet and a job, for instance.

Dick likes animals well enough, and they like him. Dogs, cats, hamsters on wheels, birds in cages. But if he had a pet, he would have to feed it, play with it, pay attention to its needs.

Best to save those energies for a rich girlfriend.

And who wants a job? Work for someone else, their schedule? Dick has a profession. Which is very different from a job.

Camosack: Victoria's Lifestyle Magazine.

Camosack is the Lekwungen word for Victoria. According to the internet, it means "Rush of Water." Richard Dock. Owner and managing editor. Also, the publisher, head writer, photographer, publicist.

The premier edition of the magazine is currently in production.

Online. Everything that is anything is online. Dick has the domain name. He just needs some advertising. Advertising dollars are the key to a successful magazine.

Along with a dynamite feature article.

The obvious choice is something on the alien moon landing, but how lame is that? Everyone is writing about aliens. And really, after *Star Wars* and *Star Trek*, what is there left to say?

Dick uses his spoon to scoop up the last of the milky sugar slurry that looks disturbingly like seminal fluid, and contemplates a line of poetry he remembers from an English class he didn't complete.

No man is an island,
Entire of itself.

Not true.
Here he is. Dick, the island. Not a part of the main.

Any man's death diminishes me,
Because I am involved in mankind.

Nope. Also, not true. Dick, the island, who doesn't much care if "a clod be washed away by the sea."

Each morning after breakfast, weather permitting, Dick walks into town. He'd drive if he had a car. But he doesn't. So, he walks. Just as well, because parking in downtown Victoria is difficult at the best of times.

And walking allows him to practise being invisible. This is easy enough to do if he stays in the condo, where no one can see him. But he has yet to master the skill in public.

Ed, whose last name Dick can never remember, is in the park by Fisherman's Wharf. Freddy the dog is with him. Freddy walks around in circles, deciding where to poop.

"How goes the magazine?"

So, Dick isn't invisible. He's not even inconspicuous.

"You should do a story on cruise ships." Ed takes a little plastic sack out of his pocket, holds it at the ready. "You see the two tankers we got in port right now?"

Dick has stood on Dallas Road across from the Ogden Point terminal and watched the ocean liners slip into port like elephant seals squeezing into girdles.

"Do an exposé on the truth about cruising." Freddy is squatting in the grass, but nothing is happening. "Disease, accidents, murder."

Dick doesn't associate cruising with murder.

"Between 2007 and 2021, there were thirty-two reported homicides and suspicious deaths." Ed makes encouraging sounds to help Freddy along. "Disasters at sea? Everyone knows the *Titanic*, but take a look at the MTS *Oceanos*, Royal Caribbean's *Explorer of the Seas*, the *Costa Concordia*, Carnival Lines' *Triumph*."

This *sounds* like a better idea than aliens on the moon. But a punchy, controversial article that criticizes a large corporation could land Dick in civil court.

"And disease?" Ed rolls his eyes. "Norovirus is the biggie. Cunard's *Queen Victoria*? Celebrity's *Constellation*? Hardly a cruise ship in service doesn't wind up with a norovirus outbreak. But you also have E. coli, salmonella, shigella, cyclospora, legionella, and everyone's new favourite, COVID. Cruise ships are floating petri dishes."

Still, Dick is a serious journalist, and a court case could also raise his profile.

"You see that new one?" says Ed. "*Napalm of the Seas*? Twenty decks, 7,600 passengers? Thing runs on liquefied natural gas. It's supposed to be 'green,' but it dumps a ton of methane into the atmosphere."

Dick likes Ed. The man is full of great information. And Dick likes Freddy, always takes the time to scratch his ears, tell him what a good dog he is.

"And if that weren't enough, now we got aliens on the moon." Ed shakes his head, rolls his eyes. "They'll probably get blamed for the heat wave in Ontario and the freak snowstorm in Alberta."

Freddy finishes his business. Dick averts his eyes, looks up. If the moon is there, he can't see it.

"Carla will have her sign out." Ed gives the baggie a spin, ties a loop with the ends, lets it hang off his little finger. "One of these days, she may even sell the old barge."

Dick leaves Ed and Freddy, crosses the park, drops down to Fisherman's Wharf. It's not so much a wharf as it is a fast-food court and a parking lot for brightly painted houseboats. Most of the businesses aren't open yet, but there are a fair number of people wandering about, taking selfies, striking poses against the water and the city skyline.

Everyone has a cellphone. Except him.

Ed is right. Carla Tupper has the For Sale sign out. She does this whenever two or more cruise ships are in port.

RIB, she calls it.

Romantic Impulse Buying.

Carla is sitting in a red lounge chair on the upper deck of her houseboat. She's dressed for the illusion of gracious living on a barge. White and yellow sundress with a soft-green straw hat, a glass of lemonade on a wicker table beside her. The houseboat looks gay in its coat of primary colours, and if you don't look closely, you can easily miss the rusting deck cleats and the alligator paint around the door frame and windows.

Dick doesn't think a tourist from Arizona is going to roll off a ship, hit the wharf on the fly, fall in love with Victoria and Carla's houseboat, and snatch it up in a moment of holiday madness.

Even if the 2016 and 2024 elections proved beyond objection that there is nothing, no matter how absurd, that Americans won't buy.

Dick has considered Carla as a possible companion. She's older than he would prefer, a little on the heavy side, and somewhat opinionated. In many ways, Carla reminds Dick of his sister, and this has cooled any enthusiasm. Still, she owns her own houseboat. If Dick sold the condo and moved in with her, he would be money to the good and could devote his full attention to the magazine.

Dick waves at Carla. Carla waves back.

So, she can see him as well.

The walk into downtown is pleasant. Erie turns into St. Lawrence, Kingston, Montreal, Quebec, Pendray, and finally Belleville. Left at Government, down the steps in front of Parliament to the sea wall, around the harbour past the Empress, up the stairs to Government Street once again, and there you are.

Downtown Victoria.

Dick likes downtown Victoria. Belleville to Herald, Wharf to Quadra. This is his world. A tight rectangle that has everything he needs. Yes, Thrifty Foods on Simcoe and the Red Barn Market on Menzies are outside these parameters, but boundaries of any sort are never perfect, and he's no pedant.

Dick pauses in front of Milano. He could have coffee here, but only if there are croissants. Today, he can see that the pastries are all gone, so he keeps going to Fisgard and the Orca.

With a quick stop at Munro's Books.

Dick doesn't buy books. And why should he? There's the library on Menzies, and a scattering of book boxes throughout the neighbourhoods, boxes where people leave their old books, boxes where people help themselves to other people's old books. A sharing of resources for the common good. An activity that has avoided the stigma of socialism.

Unlike universal health care.

Not that the books in the boxes are books Dick *wants* to read, but they are books nonetheless, and they're free. So, point made.

MUNRO'S IS THE PERFECT place to practise being invisible. It's dark and cool, with floating shadows and hidden corners. Dick imagines that people could disappear into the stacks, never be seen again.

Today, Dick stands in front of the section with the recent releases and makes a note of the books he might want to read. Author. Title. He'll pass his recommendations on to the library in James Bay. He knows they appreciate his suggestions.

Munro's is one of Dick's favourite places. Such a peaceful ambience, such a palpable sanctuary. As he wanders through the quiet but substantial stacks, he feels not only invisible but protected, confident that if a bomb were to go off in the street, the section on literary classics would shield him from harm. Or if someone shot at him, he would be able to snatch up a copy of *The Handmaid's Tale* and stop the bullet on page 316.

"Is there something I can help you find?"

Dick is startled. He feels his pleasant equilibrium slipping away.

"You can see me?"

"I can."

"You can hear me?"

"Is hearing you a problem?" asks the clerk.

Everyone wants to come to Victoria. The spring blossoms. The ocean on your doorstep. The moderate weather. The good restaurants.

Canada's Eden.

But with far too many people in the garden.

And Dick isn't just talking tourists. He has seen the figures, and they are staggering. For every person who leaves or dies, three come to take their place. All of which makes for a lively real estate market, and Dick is sure that he could sell the condo for more than he paid for it.

If he had paid for it in the first place.

Which he didn't.

Today is example enough. When he steps out of Munro's, Dick finds Government Street awash in people, a high tide of humanity, and he is forced to wade through the surf to the middle of the street.

"Don't look gloomy." A voice behind him. "How about a toonie?"

A large woman on a red access scooter pulls up alongside.

Tanis Hoplin.

"*Oh Lord, won't you buy me a burger and fries,*" Tanis sings. "*I know you got money, so tell me no lies.*"

Tanis is a regular on Government Street. Drives her electric scooter up and down the thoroughfare, doing her impersonation of Janis Joplin, who she swears is a first cousin.

"Name was originally Hoplin," Tanis tells anyone who'll listen. "She changed it 'cause everyone called her Hophead when she was a kid."

Dick has said no to Tanis hundreds of times, but it doesn't stop the woman from asking each time she sees him.

"You off for coffee?" Tanis paces him with her scooter. "I like coffee."

Dick concentrates hard on being invisible. These are the times he really needs to be invisible.

"Where you headed? Union Coffee? Bean Around the World? The Orca?" Tanis honks her horn to move a tourist out of her way. "I'm fine with a Timmies. Large. Double-double."

Dick is not going to buy Tanis coffee. He does that, and there will be no end to the insistences. If he can't manage invisible just yet, maybe he can fade a bit, lose himself in the crowd.

At the same time, he concentrates his mind on draining the battery in her scooter.

Tanis stops at View, makes a quick U-turn. This is her hunting territory. The pedestrian zone between Humboldt and View. Here, she doesn't have to worry about cars. She can concentrate on the people who move through this souvenir savanna like migrating herds of wildebeests.

"Catch you later, masturbator," she calls out after Dick.

Victoria has a fair number of street people, homeless people. They sleep in doorways. They settle over steam grates. They sack out in parks. Canada prides itself on its social policy, which, so far as Dick can see, is committed to providing electric scooters in lieu of low-income housing.

Not that a scooter is going to keep you warm in winter. Not that a scooter is going to protect you from the rain.

Dick has thought about doing a feature on Victoria's inner city and the homeless problem, but poverty and mental illness aren't all that interesting. More to the point, he'd have to interview Tanis and her scooter.

And that's not going to happen.

THE ORCA IS ON Fisgard. The place feels like an authentic coffee house, dark and intriguing. A place where poets and radicals might gather to write manifestos and plot insurrections. Dick imagines that if a revolution were to rise up and topple the power elite, it would begin in places such as this.

Dick especially likes the sign above the espresso machine.

**If you're reckless enough to trust in the sanity
and goodness of your fellow humans, you deserve to
be disappointed and slaughtered in your sleep.**

The coffee at the Orca is cheap. Dick likes that. And it's cash only. Dick likes that as well. There is an analog feel to cash only. Dick has inquired about setting up a credit account, and the woman who runs the place just stared at him, as though he were speaking Chinese. Which she should understand, because she looks Chinese. Or at least Asian. But now that Dick thinks about it, she could be Aboriginal as well.

Not that it matters.

What matters is that the Orca does not give refills. So, the revolution probably won't start here. More than likely, the revolt will begin in someone's kitchen or a garage, or in a church basement after god has been sent home for the night.

Or it won't begin at all. Real revolutions cost money. Real revolutions require commitment. People die in real revolutions. Most of the protests that Dick has seen have been objections to the loss of convenience or the curtailment of some supposed right.

Not a real revolution at all. Just a weekend forum for petty complaints.

Dick has talked to the Chinese/Aboriginal woman about his magazine, has given her a number of opportunities to buy an ad in the inaugural edition.

He's also talked with the people at Munro's and several other businesses that would benefit from the publicity of being associated with Victoria's premiere lifestyle magazine.

No one has said no, and no one has said yes. They all want to see an edition of the magazine first, which Dick sees as somewhat unreasonable and short-sighted.

Dick orders a macchiato at the counter.

"Four dollars."

"I'm Richard Dock. You probably recognize the name."

"Four dollars."

"I'm the publisher of *Camosack: Victoria's Lifestyle Magazine*."

"Four dollars."

Dick takes his macchiato to a table in a corner at the back. Near the coffee-bean roaster. From here, he can see the whole of the café, can watch the singles and the couples and the foursomes as they drink their coffee and discuss life.

The man and woman at the window table, debating e-bikes.

"What about a cargo model? Maybe the one with the extended range."

The woman is tall and solid. She reminds Dick of the professional volleyball players he's seen on the sports channel.

"They're kinda clunky, honey."

The guy is tall as well, with broad shoulders and long arms. Dick imagines that this is how he would look if he were tall with broad shoulders and long arms.

"If we got a cargo bike," says the woman, "we could use it for groceries and short-haul errands instead of the car."

"How about we get two?" says the man. "A cargo and one of those cool mountain e-bikes."

"And who would get the cool mountain bike?" asks the woman.

The older foursome at a middle table talking about ailments, doctors, operations.

"It was my gall bladder," says the woman in the green sweater. "You can't believe what a difference it made."

"Emma's cancer is back," says the man in the yellow windbreaker. "So, we're going to put the river trip off for a bit."

The second woman keeps her head down, just stares at her coffee. The muffin hasn't been touched.

"New breakthroughs in therapies every day," says the bald man in a long-sleeve shirt. "Every day."

"Aliens might have a cure," says the man in the yellow windbreaker. "If they're willing to share."

"Did you hear about the Pope?" says the bald man. "What the hell is the world coming to?"

Dick sits alone, listens to the waves of voices that ebb and flow through the room.

Electric bikes. Cancer. The new blockbuster film at the Capitol Six. The Vancouver Canucks. House prices. Raw sewage being dumped into the harbour. Immigration.

Watching people and listening to people is what makes a good journalist, and as Dick considers this, he ponders the possibility that people could be watching him, that even in the dim lighting at the back of the Orca, he might not be invisible.

Right now, they could be watching him, judging him, making up stories, hurtful stories, stories that have nothing to do with reality.

Fuck off, Dick thinks to himself. *Fuck off the lot of you.*

Did he just say that out loud?

If Dick didn't have the magazine, what would he do? This is not the first time he's asked himself this question. Okay. Easy answer. Something with the potential for profit. Something with a bit of flash, a bit of glamour. Something he could put on his dating profile to bring the cream to the top.

As he sits in the Orca and drinks his coffee, Dick runs the options once again. An elimination dance of sorts.

He can't sing. And he can't play an instrument. Darby plays the piano, so musical ability runs in the family. It just doesn't run through him.

Sports star.

Okay, basketball is out. He's too short. Baseball is out. He's too slow. Football is out. He's too small. He did try golf once, but found it remarkably difficult and frustrating, and he kept losing balls.

He could be a celebrity photographer. Follow the rich and famous around. Take photographs of actors and politicians coming out of clubs, drunk and disorderly, sell the shots to the tabloids. But cameras and lenses are expensive, and after Christopher Guerra was killed while trying to take pictures of Justin Bieber, Dick has removed "photographer" from the board.

He could be a novelist. The investment would be minimal. He already has a computer and a printer. He's read enough books to understand the general structure of a novel. And when Hollywood bought his book and turned it into a movie, he would be famous and well regarded in a quiet and sophisticated way.

He met a writer once. At a reading. At Munro's. An old guy with a grumbly voice. Tall, bent over. As though he were a winter tree in a Group of Seven landscape, weighed down by snow. There had been questions after the reading, and a woman in the audience asked him what advice he might have for young writers.

Shelter, solitude, a soft breeze.

That's what the old guy said.

Shelter, solitude, a soft breeze?

Dick walked out of the bookstore that evening wondering if the old guy had any cookies left in his jar.

Actor.

Top of his list. Even before online journalism. No equipment required. No special skills. All you need is the ability to pretend, and how hard can that be? Memorizing lines could be a challenge, but that would certainly be easier than reading music or developing an embouchure.

Of course, if he were an actor, and if he were successful, he couldn't very well be invisible. Or even obscure for that matter. Dick isn't sure how he would feel about being visible all the time, and even though being an actor is appealing, the loss of personal space might be too great.

So why not just keep doing what he does so well? Investigative journalism. Richard Dock. Editor-in-chief of *Camosack: Victoria's Lifestyle Magazine*. Invisible, but ever vigilant.

E-bikes. He could do a feature article on e-bikes.

A four-part exposé.

Start off with the pragmatic. How much would a decent e-bike set you back? Replacement tires? Replacement battery? Insurance? Cost of repairs, cost of a reliable lock?

Then move on to safety. What are the chances of being hit by a car? Are bike lanes effective? Bike-to-bike altercations? Exploding batteries? They're not just a myth.

He'd have to talk about health issues. Scraped or broken limbs from falls? A heart attack while pushing a sixty-pound e-bike home with a flat tire? Prostate cancer from sitting on a bicycle seat too long?

For people who had prostates, that is.

Dick isn't sure what the female equivalent to the prostate problem might be, but he can look it up on the internet.

And finally, the weather. Riding an e-bike around in the sunshine and ocean breezes is all well and good, but what happens when the weather turns? Rainstorms, snowstorms, high winds, freezing cold, blistering heat?

It doesn't get all that hot or cold on the coast, but global warming may change that.

Okay. There's the hard part done.

Dick finishes the coffee, takes his cup to the front. As he walks through the people sitting at tables and the people standing in line, he tries to imagine what it might be like to be famous. Being stopped for an autograph. Having your hand shaken as someone tells you how much they liked your last movie/novel/record. How many selfies with fans could he manage of a day?

Well, probably quite a few.

The Lower Causeway is crowded. People lined up to get on the whale-watching boats. People lined up for the harbour tours.

A woman with a violin is playing something that Dick doesn't recognize.

A man is sitting by himself. The sign next to him reads TALK TO A REAL PERSON.

Two women are standing patiently next to a display of pamphlets. Dick wonders if they can see him, is tempted to stop and ask.

"That's a great hat." The older woman steps forward. "Can you tell me where you got it?"

"My husband would love a hat like that," says the younger woman.

Dick touches the brim of his hat, puts on his worldly face. The two women move in on either side.

"You look like someone who is concerned with the state of the world," says the older woman.

"And God has good news." The younger woman hands him a pamphlet.

The women are much too close. He's seen the nature shows. He's seen the African wild dogs take down an antelope. He's seen the killer whales beach themselves to grab a seal.

"And we can all use good news."

Dick touches his hat a second time, pushes forward, doesn't look back. Let them find someone else to eat.

THERE'S A RALLY IN front of the Parliament Buildings. Most weekends, there is a gathering of some sort or other. A few years back, truckers had shown up to protest intelligence, good sense, and gun control.

That had been unpleasant.

Horns were honked. Engines were revved. All day, all night.

Each day, there were threats that the big rigs were going to be driven through the doors of government.

Dick had come down several times to watch the protest. The disruption went on for almost a month, and then the police finally moved in. Little was accomplished. Hard words. Frayed tempers. Wasted gas.

Today, the topic is high mortgage rates and pay raises for provincial legislators. There are the usual bullhorns, placards, drums, whistles, cowbells. Shouted slogans in a call-and-answer cadence.

"What do we want?"

"Justice."

"When do we want it?"

"Now!"

Dick can see the potential in a business that rents sound equipment to protesters.

There's a troupe of seniors in yellow T-shirts with a slogan on the front that Dick can't read. A small anti-abortion group has set up a display with graphic photos. There's an ice-cream truck at the curb, along with a hot-dog vendor's cart. Off to the side is a knot of people with placards that say WELCOME ALIENS.

The police have Belleville blocked off between Government and Menzies, as they generally do. The sun is shining, and everyone is having a good time.

By the time Dick gets to Oswego, the tourists have disappeared, and he has the street to himself. That's the beauty of Victoria. The crowds are concentrated around the harbour, on Government Street, in Chinatown. Yes, Fisherman's Wharf gets its share of people, but it's somewhat out of the way and visitors from elsewhere have to be determined to get there.

Frankly, it's not worth the effort.

And so, just before noon, on a lovely summer day, Dick is back in his one-bedroom condo, in time for lunch.

There's just enough chili left. He'll stop by the Red Barn and pick up another carton. Dick is perfectly capable of cooking for himself, but with his busy schedule, takeout is the perfect solution for the working professional.

He's also getting low on sourdough bread and tomatoes. And fruit. He's going to have to get more fruit.

If it's not one thing, it's another.

Dick has just put the chili into the microwave and set the timer when there's a knock at his door. This is a bit unnerving. His sister is in Ontario, and he hasn't buzzed anyone into the building.

Dick looks through the fish eye. The woman standing in the hall looks familiar. He's fairly sure she lives in the building, but he can't remember her name.

Tanya, Tammy, Teresa.

"Hi," she says. "Miranda Lansky? Two floors up?"

"Of course." Dick doesn't remember Miranda.

"We met at the association meeting last year?"

"Right." Dick doesn't remember the meeting either.

"I don't want to bother you, but I'm hoping I can encourage you to come tonight."

Dick waits.

"As I'm sure you know," says Miranda, "a good many of the units are being turned into Vrbo and Airbnb rentals. If we don't put a stop to it, we'll lose our community, and the building will turn into a hotel. No one wants that."

"No one," says Dick.

"So, I can count on you?"

"Absolutely," says Dick. "Absolutely."

"Sometimes I forget," says Miranda. "So I set an alarm on my cellphone as a reminder. Maybe you should do the same."

Dick is not happy to be reminded that he doesn't have a cell-phone.

"Then I'll see you there?"

Dick thanks Miranda, says his goodbyes, closes the door, locks it.

He's heard of Vrbo and Airbnb. He's even considered renting out the condo. He could use the extra money. But where would he go? Strangers in his space? Going through his drawers, snooping in his private spaces?

He'd probably have to move all his clothes and put anything valuable into storage. What if the renters threw a big party and wrecked the unit? There have certainly been stories about that kind of misbehaviour. And where would he go? A hotel in town could well be more expensive than the rent he'd receive.

The more he thinks about people prowling about in his condo, the more he sympathizes with Miranda. He wouldn't care to see the Lagoon turned into a short-term rental with unwashed guests roaming the hallways like a troupe of baboons.

Maybe he will go to the meeting. Most likely, there will be free coffee. He could share a cup with Miranda. She's not the kind of rich girlfriend he has in mind. A little too tall with limp, mousy-brown hair and thin lips. But she might be pleasant companionship while he waits for his dating application to be approved.

The microwave dings. The chili is done. Lunch is served.

As he eats, he makes notes in his head. Now that he thinks about it, e-bikes would make for a boring article. The only advantage that he can see is that you don't have to pedal as hard to get where you want to go. Yes, e-bikes would be great for old people who don't have the energy or stamina of a twenty-year-old, but do you really want a herd of octogenarians wobbling about the streets, running into cars, knocking pedestrians over?

And who really cares about bikes, e or otherwise? Bike riders. That's it. And are there enough of them to appreciate the work Dick might put into an article? Are any of them inclined to take out an ad in his magazine?

Ed is right. Better to do an article on cruising. More people do that, and there's more scope for interesting stories and disasters. A virulent outbreak of a killer disease. The sinking of a luxury liner. Murder on the high seas.

Don't get that kind of drama riding a bike around Victoria.

All right. Decision made. E-bikes out. Cruises in.

THE WALK OUT TO Dallas Road and the terminals is pleasant. Dick takes his time, imagines himself a *flâneur*, a well-dressed rogue from an old black and white movie, set in Paris in the early twentieth century. He really needs a silver-handled cane, a pencil-thin moustache, and a fedora set at a rakish angle to complete the illusion, but he makes do with a jaunty gait and a nonchalant swing to his arms.

Step, slide, step, slide, swing, swing, swing.

Ed's witticisms aside, the two ships in port are *Norwegian Star* and *Splendour of the Seas*. And they are enormous. Even from a distance, they are enormous. Dick tries to think of an appropriate metaphor with which to describe them. A clever phrase that could be the lead for the article.

Crisis in Cruising has nice alliteration but is needlessly vague.

Murder on the Main. More alliteration but too much on point.

Tears Before the Mast is nicely literary, but how many people know Richard Henry Dana?

Time to uncover the truth behind luxury cruises. He's heard the rumours, of course. Water parks, gift shops, restaurants, spas.

Vegas-style floor shows, casinos, go-kart racing, skydiving, skeet shooting.

But Dick needs to see all of this for himself, needs to wander about, peek into the staterooms, sit in a deck chair, stand at the bow and feel the wind in his hair.

Two ships in port. Worth a try? Is he feeling lucky today? Yes, he is.

There's a line of people standing by the security fence. Overweight, walking shorts, polo shirts, straw hats, ill-advised footwear. They have lanyards around their necks with a plastic card clipped to the end.

Dick supposes that these are passengers.

They take turns stepping through the security gate and touching their cards to a security reader. Dick doesn't have a card, and he can see that getting on one of the ships is not going to be as easy as he had supposed.

There is a guard posted at the gate. This is good news. Dick waits for the line to clear, so he can talk to the woman in private, explain who he is, why he requires a tour of the ship.

She looks to be intelligent and understanding.

Only she's not.

Dick shows her his business card, rolls the name of the magazine around in his mouth, as though he were sucking on candy, suggests that when his photographer arrives, he might want to use a photograph of her for the article.

Talking to a stone. No card. No entrance. No exceptions.

The guard is not particularly attractive. This is part of the problem. Unattractive women, in Dick's experience, are uncooperative. He's not sure why this is true. It simply is.

"*Camosack?*" says Dick. "You must have heard of it. It's a major magazine. M.A.J.O.R."

"I don't make the rules."

"Why don't we talk to someone in charge?"

"I am in charge."

"Someone with authority."

The guard smiles, keys the mic clipped to her shoulder. "Security," she says in an authoritative voice, "10-66, front gate."

THERE'S A PEDESTRIAN LANE that cuts in from Dallas Road to the corner of St. Lawrence and Niagara. Dick is almost there when a man catches up to him.

"Excuse me."

The man is about Dick's age. Same height, weight. Same mousy-brown hair. Same glasses. For a moment, Dick feels as though he's looking in a mirror.

"Heard you talking to the guard," says the man. "You really with a magazine?"

The man is dressed in shorts, polo shirt. A lanyard and a plastic card hang around his neck.

"I am."

"And you're doing a story on cruises?"

"I am."

"I'm Stan, Stanley Bulger. I'm on the *Splendour of the Seas.*"

Now that Dick is up close, he can see that Stanley hasn't shaved in a couple of days, can see that his eyes are wet and red.

Splendour of the Seas is enormous. Dick can see why Ed is concerned.

Stanley glances back at the port. "One hundred and seventy-three nights. Eight wonders of the world, sixty countries. The cruise of a lifetime."

Dick whistles. He can't help himself. That's almost a year.

Stanley nods. "My fiancée broke up with me. Like I'd been hit by a train. So, I said what the fuck, get out of Dodge. Pick up the pieces. Hit the reset button."

Dick can't even begin to imagine how much such a cruise would cost.

"I'm filthy rich," says Stanley. "Digital marketing. So, what do you want to know?"

For the next half-hour, Stanley regales Dick with stories of the cruise. So far as he knows, there have been no murders aboard.

"But I've got a suite on the top deck. Don't hear too much about what's happening in steerage."

And disease? Dick wants to know if the ship has had an outbreak.

"Trip before us," says Stanley, "everyone was puking up a storm. But they gave the barge a good cleaning, and so far, so good."

Dick enjoys talking with Stanley. It's like talking to himself.

"There's a bunch of pools and hot tubs, and water slides. You can rock climb, skydive, surf, do some skeet shooting." Stanley runs a hand through his hair. "There's a casino, and you can shop till you drop."

Dick tries to imagine how you would skydive on a cruise ship.

"But you'd think for the money, the food would be better. I mean, there's tons of it everywhere. You can't turn around without running into food. It's just not anything special."

And nightly entertainment?

"Hard pass," says Stanley. "Not my thing. Amity would love it."

Dick can see that Stanley misses Amity. He wonders if she's a rich girlfriend like the ones he wants to meet.

"We were going to get married. You know, have kids. Happy ever after."

Dick makes a sympathetic noise.

"Yeah," says Stanley, "I know I look like shit. You know why she broke it off?"

Women. Dick sighs. Who knows how they think.

Stanley looks up into the sky. "It was the aliens."

Dick tries to imagine the problems the aliens might create in a personal relationship.

"I'm joking. Wasn't the aliens. Amity said I'm too full of myself, that there's no room in my life for her." Stanley's face softens. "And you know what? She's probably right."

Dick wants to suggest that Stanley should shave, that he'll feel much better after a hot shower.

"Ship is in port for two nights. Going to see the sights. Maybe I'll see you around."

Dick agrees that this is possible.

"Here's my info." Stanley hands him a card. "Appreciate it if you'd send me a copy of your article."

THE REST OF THE day is spent floating. Dick floats over to Thrifty Foods. Bananas, grapes, tomatoes, sourdough bread, cottage cheese, chicken thighs, a pound cake. He floats to the library. Is the new Mick Herron novel in? Daniel Silva?

Floats to South Turner, sails up and down the street. Have any of the houses he'd like to buy come on the market? He's going to talk to Darby again about selling the condo and buying a single-family house in a good neighbourhood.

The strata fees on the condo are absurd.

Thank god he isn't paying them.

And then he floats home, opens Google, looks up information on e-bikes. If the cruise line people are going to be recalcitrant, why should he bother to give them free publicity in his magazine?

So, cruises are out. E-bikes back in. And the good news is that he has already done most of the research. All he has left is a couple of paragraphs on the cost of an e-bike and the health hazards for women, which, he learns on Google, include yeast and urinary tract infections, saddle sores, and vaginal numbness.

Dick is disappointed to discover that the hazards for women are not all that serious.

He revisits the question of e-bikes versus regular bikes. He's done this before, but Dick has found that it never hurts to re-examine your research.

When he first looked into the question of e-bikes, he was surprised to discover that regular bikes sell for the same price as e-bikes. Now he understands why. Regular bikes are built out of lighter and more expensive materials. They have better, more precise gears. E-bikes, on the other hand, are made out of heavier, less expensive materials, the cost being in the batteries and the motors.

You can get cheap regular bikes and cheap e-bikes, and you can get expensive models of both. In the end, they all do the same thing. The choice seems to revolve around image, around what you want the bike to say about who you are.

All of which leaves Dick with the annoying question that he can't avoid. If you're contemplating buying an e-bike, why not get a scooter? An electric scooter can go most of the same places as an e-bike, and there's no pedalling required. But if you're going to get a scooter, why not get a car?

More to the point, if you're going to go the traditional route and spend a couple thousand dollars on a regular bike with all the pedalling required, why not buy a cellphone, keep the change, and walk?

This could be the surprise question in the article, the environmental turn. Bikes of any sort versus walking. The philosophical element that makes *Camosack* worth the reading.

THAT EVENING, DICK REMEMBERS the condo association meeting. By the time he gets to the community centre room on the fourth floor, the Vrbo/Airbnb question has already turned into a rough and tumble affair. Dick had no idea just how contentious the matter could be. Nor did he realize that almost half of the units in the building are already owned by large holding companies.

"See the guy in the suit." Miranda points to a heavy-set man with a three-day stubble beard. "Lawyer."

Dick has considered an article on men's facial hair, so he is familiar with circle beards, royale beards, goatees and petite goatees, Van Dykes, anchor beards, Balbo beards, and the difference between a horseshoe moustache and a gunslinger.

"Guy represents most of the absentee landlords."

Absentee landlord. Dick can't help it. The term sounds like something out of *Game of Thrones*. The Landlord of James Bay. The Master of Erie. The Lord of the Wharf.

"He's going to vote against any attempt to control short-term rentals."

The lawyer looks like Tony Soprano. If Soprano had facial hair. Dick wonders if the man is armed. If this were New Jersey, he would be.

"Strangers coming and going every week?" says Miranda. "Who wants to live in a hotel?"

A Room with a View. The Night of the Iguana. The Best Exotic Marigold Hotel. The Grand Budapest Hotel. Dick thinks of the movies he's seen that feature people living in hotels.

The Shining.

"Never knowing your neighbour. No sense of community."

The debate is lively with threats of penalties and lawsuits, and the meeting ends with a motion to carry the discussion over to the next meeting.

Dick votes in favour.

Miranda catches him at the coffee pot.

"You should join us on the roof," she says. "Warren is setting up his telescope. We're going to look at the moon."

Dick helps himself to a chocolate-chip cookie and an oatmeal raisin.

"If the sky is clear," says Miranda, "Warren says we might be able to see the alien ship."

The cookies are store-bought, and they're stale.

"You should do a story on the aliens," says Miranda. "Warren thinks they're responsible for all the seafoam in Tofino."

Dick takes two more cookies, slips away back to his apartment. Locks the door. Turns off the lights. Settles into being invisible again.

He's not going to go to the roof to look at the moon, and he's not going to waste his time on aliens. No one to interview. No exclusive photographs. No information on Google. What kind of a lame article would that be?

Dick hasn't got time for such folly. He has a feature to write. He has a magazine to get out. And while he's waiting for inspiration to show itself, he'll finish his profile for the dating sites.

Annual income?

Relationship status?

Tell us about yourself. Maximum of 2,000 words.

Please attach a current photograph.

Richard Dock, Dick to his family. Financially secure. Unattached, but open to a stable, long-term relationship. Likes to travel.

Dick will have to research the travel question. Do rich women go on cruises or do they just fly to where they want to go?

It's midnight before he's able to think of good answers to the questions. He hopes he's gotten all of them right. Afterwards, he sits on the balcony with a small bowl of grapes, watches the moon float in the night sky.

Maybe he shouldn't have been so cavalier about the aliens. Someone is going to be the first to tell their story. Someone is going to be the first to introduce them to the world. Why not him?

But first, what he really needs is a cellphone.

IV

Morning, and another day at Autumn Leaves. Thea gets out of bed, goes to the bathroom to pee, brush her teeth, wipe her underarms with a washcloth. Tomorrow, she'll shower. She's on her way to the dining room when the phone on her nightstand rings.

Nico calls her every week, but not every day. She's sorry she didn't have a daughter. A daughter would call more often. A daughter would understand.

"Hello," says a woman, her English accented in a manner that reminds Thea of the characters in *Slumdog Millionaire*. "We are cleaning the ducts in your neighbourhood."

"I don't have any dirty ducts," Thea starts, as she always does, "but I've got some really filthy geese."

"We will send someone to accomplish your ducts as they may need cleaning?"

"Geese," said Thea, repeating the punchline. "Do you clean geese?"

The people who clean ducts never stay on the line after this, but Thea doesn't mind. At least they have the courtesy to call in person. So much better than the recorded calls about the unauthorized activity on her Amazon account or the problems with her Visa card that require immediate action.

She doesn't have an Amazon account, and she doesn't have a Visa card. Do these people think she's senile? Do they think her head zips up the back?

Evidently, her son does.

This is the only explanation as to why Nico dumped her here like a bag of yard waste. Yes, she's eighty-seven, but so what? Lots of people this age live on their own.

Okay, so she had to give up her car. And sure, she is having some difficulty with her vision. She even had a fall, but that was because she had allowed herself to get too hungry and her blood sugars took a plunge. Everyone falls at one time or other. What matters is that you're able to get up.

She certainly didn't need the ambulance.

But even if you view these separate and unrelated details as some sort of downward spiral, it doesn't excuse the alacrity with which Nico moved her out of her house.

Her house, her house, her house.

There was the matter of the fire on the stove, but there had been a reasonable explanation for that.

"Mrs. Karras?"

It's the new girl, the one with the glasses that don't suit her face. And the ugly shoes. Donna or Diane or Dolly.

"The Paradise Mall? Van will be here in ten minutes. Are you joining us today?"

Of course she'll be joining them. It's Saturday, the day when many of the businesses set up tables in the main concourse with special deals and samples.

Thea is not about to miss that.

"And we're not going to wander off, are we?"

THE MOBILITY VAN IS crowded. Thea has to sit next to Joan Payne.

"They always send the old bus." Joan takes the window. "The seats are hard, and they keep the air conditioner at twenty-four degrees to save gas."

Thea tries sitting sideways with her legs in the aisle. She considers standing. Her knees are already stiff and aching. Her arm is sore as well. From where the nurse at the hospital took blood.

Was that yesterday or the day before?

"Did you hear that Blessica is going back to Quezon?" Joan rolls her eyes. "But that doesn't make any sense, because if her baby was born here, it would be a Canadian citizen."

Joan's hips begin to spread out on the seat like a mudslide.

"I'm sure Quezon is nice, but you don't see people lining up in Toronto to take out Philippine citizenship."

If they don't get to the mall in good order, Thea is going to wind up on the floor.

"If you ask me, all this unrest can be laid at the feet of the aliens." Joan sits up a little straighter, rearranges her left buttock. "If they even have feet. No one has actually seen one, have they? I mean they could be bowls of green Jell-O for all we know."

For the past week, Nora Blotterton, who has the room across the hall from Thea, has been insisting that the aliens are killing off the elderly with a chemical they're putting in bottled water.

"You drink the stuff," Nora told Thea, "and when you reach a certain age, poof, you drop dead."

Thea has never been a fan of bottled water.

"Remember Orem Clarke? That's all he drank, and look what happened to him."

Nico has concerns about the aliens. It's one of the reasons he gives for not wanting her to stay in her house.

"We need to wait to see what the aliens plan to do."

"The aliens aren't going to care where I live."

"The U.S. and Russia are talking about the possibility of a full-scale war. That happens, and there would be no point in having a house."

"We should all move back to Greece," Thea told Nico. "We could buy a nice house in Kymi, and you could find a nice wife."

"I have a nice wife, Mom," said Nico. "And there's no way I'm moving to Greece."

"My father came from Greece."

"Sure, Mom," Nico said each time the subject came up, "that was *pappous*. That's not us."

"And if we were back in Greece," Thea said, her voice brimming with conviction, "we wouldn't have to worry about aliens."

BY THE TIME THEY get to the mall, the place is crowded, and all the electric carts are taken. Joan is not happy.

"You would think they could get more carts," she says. "This isn't Mexico."

The new girl with the bad glasses and the ugly shoes is wearing her name tag. She's not Donna or Diane or Dolly. She's Tabby.

"You can use the walker," Tabby tells Joan. "It will be good exercise."

"I'm just going to sit here until you find me an electric cart."

"Give the walker a try. You might like it."

"You're too young to be deaf," says Joan, and she sits down on the edge of the fountain.

This is Thea's chance to escape. Whenever they come to the mall, Joan wants Thea to stay by her side.

"We're the two musketeers," Joan likes to say. "One for all, and all for one."

In Joan's case, Thea reminds herself, the "one" and the "all" Joan is talking about is Joan.

"I'm going to walk around a little." Thea ignores Joan and the corn on her little toe, and limps off toward the food court.

"Stay with me," Joan shouts, the demand in her voice hard and brittle, a hammer on plate glass. "You can walk later. After I get my cart."

Thea wonders what the aliens do with their elderly. She assumes that they have sex of some sort or another, that they have children, that they grow old and die. It would hardly be fair if they didn't. So far as she knows, no one has raised those particular issues. There was the report in one of the tabloids Tabby brought back to Autumn Leaves from the supermarket that featured an eyewitness report of the Blackfoot and the aliens having sex on the Alberta prairies.

"They could be trying to start a completely new race," Tabby told her. "To replace us."

"And not a moment too soon."

"You can joke, Mrs. Karras," Tabby had said, "but miscegenation is serious business."

THE WALK HURTS HER little toe more than she expected, and Thea has to take little breaks in front of store windows. Aldo is having a sale on plastic sandals. Bath & Body Works has a special on gift packages tied up with bright ribbon. Bentley's summer collection of luggage is on display.

Thea stops in front of the LensCrafters store. There's a large sign in the window that says ALIENS SPECIAL. Thea hadn't considered that the aliens might need glasses, but it stands to reason that as they age, so would their eyes.

If they have eyes.

LensCrafters isn't alone. A number of stores have signs in their windows welcoming the aliens. Starbucks, Virgin Mobile, Shoppers Drug Mart, Roots, Pier 1 Imports, Foot Locker.

The latest rage in weekend mall business is pop-up booths. The last time they came, Joan dragged Thea to one that was selling face creams guaranteed to remove the bags from beneath your eyes.

"It'll take fifteen years off your face," the young man told Joan.

The man was younger than Nico, though not as sturdily built as her son. And whoever cut his hair needed to reconsider that profession. The sides of the man's head had been shaved while the top had been left to go to seed in a weedy clump that flopped about as he talked.

"All this puffy and slumping skin," the young man said, touching Joan's face, "will simply disappear."

The man rubbed a white lotion onto the skin under one of Joan's eyes, so she could see the before and the after. Thea had to admit that the stuff did tighten the skin and reduce the bag.

"So, which eye do you like?" the man had asked. "Which eye is the real you?"

There had been a special on the gift box that day. Only $345, normally a $900 value. A savings of $555. "Try it for a week," the man had said. "If you don't like it, bring it back for a full refund."

THEA GETS A CHOCOLATE from Purdy's that she saves in a bag for later. So she can eat it in front of Joan.

"Have you ever been to African Lion Safari?"

It takes a moment for Thea to realize the woman is talking to her.

"Canada's original safari adventure." The woman is standing in front of a table that is covered with brochures and photographs. "One of the top ten destinations in Ontario."

Thea has heard of the place. "What number is it?"

"What?"

"What number is it?" Thea asks again. "Is it number one or number six or number ten?"

"Some people think it's a zoo," says the woman. "But it's not."

"I'm guessing Niagara Falls is number one," says Thea, "and I hear the aquarium in Toronto is interesting."

"African Lion Safari is a game park," says the woman. "The animals roam free. The people are in cages."

Thea smiles to herself. If the woman wants to talk about cages, she should come to Autumn Leaves.

"You're in your car," says the woman. "Or a tour bus. So, it's completely safe."

Now Thea remembers why she knows about the place. "Didn't a tiger eat a couple of people?"

"No one was eaten." The woman turns bright red. "There was an unfortunate incident where two people were scratched."

Thea has been scratched by Mr. Boots, the house cat at Autumn Leaves. She tries to imagine what a tiger would do.

"We run tours to African Lion Safari."

"From here?"

"Every Saturday and Sunday for the season," says the woman. "Would you like a brochure?"

Thea takes the brochure. She'll give it to Joan. Maybe Joan will go on the tour. Thea tries to imagine a tiger dragging Joan out through the window of a bus. It would have to be a big window. It would have to be a big tiger.

"Our next tour leaves in half an hour," says the woman. "And if you sign up now, I can offer you a fifteen-percent discount."

"Is there an age limit?"

"Absolutely not," says the woman. "We've had a ninety-seven-year-old man take the tour. He said he wanted to see the kangaroos jump before he died."

"African Lion Safari has kangaroos?"

"Reds and western greys," says the woman.

"I thought kangaroos were only in Australia," says Thea.

"They're in New Guinea as well," says the woman. "All the way back from the park, he couldn't stop talking about the experience."

"So, he died happy."

"He's probably still alive," says the woman. "He just went last week."

Over the top of her glasses, Thea can see Joan barrelling down the mall toward her in an electric cart.

"We have group rates," says the woman. "Ten or more, and you get a really good discount."

Joan catches Thea just before the food court.

"You should have waited for me," says Joan. "You know what happens when you wander off on your own."

"Where's Donna?"

"Never mind Tabby," says Joan. "Are we going to eat?"

Thea isn't particularly hungry.

"Because I'm hungry," says Joan, "and I don't want to eat at that Asian place with the noodles and vegetables."

"I may go to African Lion Safari."

Joan doesn't hear Thea the first time, and Thea has to tell her again.

"African Lion Safari," says Joan. "Are you crazy? Not too long ago, a guy got crushed by an elephant."

"They have kangaroos. Have you ever seen a kangaroo?"

Joan aims her cart at New York Fries. "Of course I've seen kangaroos."

"I mean actual live kangaroos," says Thea. "Seeing animals on television isn't the same."

Joan orders a large fries and a quarter-pound premium hot dog. "What's wrong with seeing animals on television? You think anyone wants to see the aliens in person?"

Thea hasn't spent much time wondering about the aliens and how they look. She's more concerned about getting out of Autumn Leaves and back into her own house.

"I can tell you," says Joan, "I'd rather see them on television."

"Maybe they're beautiful."

"No," says Joan. "If they were beautiful, they would have already shown themselves. The reason we haven't seen them is that they're hideous and probably smell bad."

Joan has Thea take her hot dog to the condiment bar and load it up with everything, mustard, relish, ketchup, and hot peppers.

"Don't skimp on the ketchup," Joan tells Thea.

While Joan eats her hot dog and fries, Thea reads the brochure on African Lion Safari. In addition to the animals in the game park, there's a water park with slides, and a petting zoo with llamas and goats and rabbits. The more she reads, the more she thinks she would like African Lion Safari.

Especially if she were twelve.

If the aliens can travel all this way, Thea reasons, perhaps they can change time, and she could be twelve again. Just for a day. But would she go to African Lion Safari or would she use her turned-back time to do something else? A date with Harold Fields perhaps, though then she should probably ask to be seventeen.

At least.

Joan had shown her an article in *Reader's Digest* that insisted you could stay young if you believed you were young, that age is a state of mind. All Thea has to do is look at the skin on her arms to know that that piece of advice is bullshit.

"I may have to get another hot dog," says Joan. "You should get something to eat."

"Not hungry."

"If you get an order of fries," says Joan, "I'll split them with you."

Thea checks her watch. She still has time to make the tour if she wants.

Joan begins to giggle. "I was just thinking. What if that's what we are?"

Thea checks the menu above the New York Fries kiosk to see if they serve anything that is not deep-fried.

"I mean what if we're African Lion Safari?"

What Thea discovers when she looks at the menu is that she really does need a new pair of glasses.

"What if that's how the aliens see us?"

The last time she got new glasses, Nico had insisted that she keep her old frames. Maybe this time her cheap son will take her to a place with all the new designer brands.

"Look around," says Joan. "What do you see?"

Thea helps herself to one of Joan's fries.

"Animals," says Joan. "Just a bunch of animals."

If her son isn't going to move her back into her house, the least he can do is buy her new frames, frames that complement her face, frames that make her look and feel younger.

"Those kids over there?" Joan points what's left of her hot dog at a group of teenagers clustered around one of the mobile phone booths. "Monkeys."

Maybe something metallic. In a bright colour.

"And those women in sweat clothes? A herd of elephants."

Bright red or a deep copper. With adjustable nose pads.

"I'm a lion," says Joan, "and you're a water buffalo."

When she first got it, Thea hadn't liked the idea of a hearing aid. But the more time she spends with Joan, the more she has come to appreciate the options it offers.

"Maybe the aliens will put us in a wildlife refuge," says Joan. "Or in a concentration camp."

Thea reaches up and finds the volume control on her hearing aid.

"Or on a reserve like the Indians." Joan uses a finger to scoop out the last of the poutine. "You should watch the History Channel more often. Just because we're old doesn't mean we can't learn things."

Joan doesn't order another hot dog, because she has to go to the bathroom. "You need to come with me," she says.

"I don't have to go to the bathroom."

"That's not the point," says Joan. "It's what friends do, and I need someone to watch my cart."

"You have a key," says Thea. "No one can use it without a key."

"And if you see anyone trying to take it, just scream like hell."

THEA WAITS UNTIL JOAN has locked herself in the stall before she walks out of the bathroom and heads back to the African Lion Safari booth. The woman is still there, but she's packing up the brochures.

"Is it too late to get on the tour?" Thea asks.

"I'm afraid it is," says the woman, "but you could go next week."

"Could be dead by next week," says Thea. "I hear the aliens want to start a war."

"I heard that too," says the woman, "but so far, they haven't done much of anything."

"Don't they want us to get rid of all our nuclear weapons?"

"I meant anything bad."

Thea is disappointed that she has missed the tour. It's all Joan's fault, and she secretly hopes that someone does take her cart.

"Do you have your own house?"

"Here." The woman hands Thea a CD in a blue plastic case. "It's an overview of the game park. If you aren't able to take the tour, at least you'll be able to see what it looks like."

"If you had the chance to live in Greece, would you take it?"

"Probably not," says the woman. "I don't speak Italian."

JOAN IS PARKED IN the middle of the mall, next to a bench, talking with another woman.

"Where'd you go?" she says when she sees Thea. "I told you to stay and guard the cart."

The other woman is pudgy with hair that hangs off her head like a wet mop.

"This is Tina," says Joan. "She's over at Sundown Mansion."

"Lena," says the woman. "Sunset Manor. It's the new gated adult community."

Thea sits on the bench. One of the reasons that Joan comes to the mall is to find someone who hasn't heard her stories.

"She's seen aliens," says Joan.

"It was from a distance," says Lena. "Out in the parking lot."

Thea watches television, so she knows that there have been any number of people who say they have seen aliens. Thea figures it's wishful thinking, coupled with mass hysteria.

"What were they doing?"

"Just standing there," says Lena. "Five or six of them."

Joan leans on the handlebars. "What did they look like?"

"Meldon says their plan is to kidnap a bunch of us," says Lena, "take us back to the mother ship for interrogation."

Thea plays along. "Interrogate us about what?"

"I don't know," says Lena. "How the government works?"

"No one knows how the government works," says Joan. "I think they're here to observe us."

"Like a zoo?" says Lena. "That makes sense."

"Absolutely." Joan turns to Thea. "Tell Tina about African Lion Safari."

"Meldon and I went there last year," says Lena. "Our son took us."

"Tina has a husband," says Joan, by way of explanation.

"Sixty years and counting," says Lena.

"I've had three." Joan taps the horn on the cart. "Killed them all."

"They say it's not a zoo," says Lena, "that the animals are able to roam free."

Thea unfolds the brochure and lays it out on the bench. There's not much information. Mostly the coloured pictures are there for encouragement.

"Meldon looked it up on Wikipedia," says Lena. "It's 750 acres, so, there's free and there's free."

"Sort of like Autumn Leaves."

"Well, you have to figure on fences at some point," says Lena. "You don't want a herd of zebra on the 401."

"Wouldn't that be something," says Joan. "You're toddling along on your way to Toronto for a nice dinner, and wham, you run into a dozen elephants."

"It's not completely safe." Lena lowers her voice and leans in to Joan. "A young man was crushed by an elephant, and a couple was mauled by a Bengal tiger, and another guy was attacked by another elephant."

Thea folds the brochure up, drops it into the garbage can next to the bench.

"When we went," says Lena, "Meldon made sure that we stayed clear of the elephants."

Thea eases herself off the bench, slides into Joan's blind spot, drifts away from the two women. Up ahead, herds of people are in motion. They amble past windows filled with dresses and sports coats and jewellery and eyeglasses and chocolate, congregate in the shade of sidewalk restaurants and coffee shops.

The human zoo. Thea smiles at the thought. African Lion Safari and the Paradise Mall. Thea watched a show on octopuses, watched the animals slip in and out of impossible situations. If she were an octopus, she'd slither back to her house, slide in behind the dishwasher.

That would show Nico not to underestimate his mother.

Thea steadies herself and heads down the mall. In the distance, she can see the front entrance. All she has to do is keep moving, hit the doors, and break out into the light.

The week after the aliens landed on the moon, the prime minister announces that the Pope is going to visit Canada. Bria's grandmother takes her to one side.

"Not the rosary story again."

"You're the one who has to do it," says her grandmother.

"It's stupid."

"It was your great-grandmother's dying request."

"I didn't even know her."

"She held you when you were a baby."

"No, she didn't," says Bria. "She was dead way before I was born."

Bria knows the story by heart. Her great-grandmother Florence Neeposh sent away to St. Anne's residential school at age six. Confined there for ten years in the care of the Grey Nuns of Montreal for the offence of being Indian. The beatings, the humiliations, the assault on self-esteem, the terrible food, the frightful living conditions. All in the name of god, the Catholic Church, and the federal government.

"You know, you were named after your great-grandmother."

"No, I wasn't."

"I wanted to name you Florence," says her grandmother. "Your mother wanted to call you Helen. Your father wanted to call you Maria. In the end, we all had to compromise."

There was a priest from Montreal who would come to St. Anne's every so often with special rosaries that he gave to special girls.

"Those rosaries," says her grandmother, "were blessed by the Pope himself."

"There's a word for creeps like that."

Bria's grandmother goes to her dresser drawers and takes out a wood box that once held two pounds of Kraft Canadian cheese from Outremont, Quebec. Bria used to snoop through the box when she was little, so she knows what's in there.

"It's an heirloom."

For instance, Bria knows that her grandmother keeps earrings in the cheese box. And a small beaded coin purse. And some porcupine quills. And a gold chain. And a handful of coins from Mexico and the U.S. And a wristwatch that no longer keeps time.

And the special rosary for special girls.

"The beads are made out of cedar of Lebanon." Bria's grandmother lays the rosary out on the table. "Nowadays, they make them out of plastic."

Bria braces herself for what she knows is going to come next. Bria's grandmother picks the rosary up, lets it dangle from her fingers.

"I'm too old, so you have to go."

"What about Mom?"

"Your mother's too busy," says Bria's grandmother. "And she's not Cree. She's Irish."

"That sounds racist to me," says Bria.

"There's Cree business," says Bria's grandmother, "and there's Irish business."

"Then get Dad to do it."

"It has to be a woman."

"And that's sexist."

Bria's grandmother sets the rosary back on the table. "These things have to be done properly. Otherwise, they're not worth doing."

"Then don't do them," says Bria.

The rosary is still on the table when everyone sits down to eat.

"That Florence's rosary?" says Bria's father.

"It is," says Bria's grandmother.

"The one with the scratches on the back?"

That's part of the rosary story. The scratches on the back of the crucifix. Four scratches with a diagonal line through them and then four more scratches by themselves.

Nine.

Whatever the scratches are supposed to represent, the count is nine.

"Number of times she was raped." Bria has said this before, but it still annoys her mother.

"Bria!"

"We don't know that for sure," says her father.

"My mother never said," says Bria's grandmother, "but you have to assume it was something unpleasant."

"Maybe some sort of corporal punishment," says Bria's father. "The Grey Nuns were famous for that."

"There was an electric chair at St. Anne's," says Bria's mother. "It could have been the electric chair."

Bria helps herself to another plate of mac and cheese. "Just stick it in an envelope and mail it to Rome."

Bria's grandmother shakes her head. "Not the same thing. Your great-grandmother wanted to return the rosary to the Pope in person."

Bria pushes the rosary to one side. "What's for dessert?"

On Saturday, Bria and her best friend, Tabby Marcotte, go to the farmers' market to get some of the little made-while-you-wait doughnuts that the Mennonites sell.

"My dad still won't help me get a car," says Tabby. "He acts like I'm nineteen."

"You are nineteen."

"Twenty next week," says Tabby. "It doesn't have to be a new car."

"You should get one of those electric bikes."

"I'd rather crawl," says Tabby.

Bria gets a basket of peaches. When she opens her purse to pay the woman at the stand, there is the rosary.

"You Catholic?"

"No," says Bria. "It's my grandmother's idea of a joke."

"Your grandmother Catholic?"

"No," says Bria. "It was my great-grandmother's."

"Cool," says Tabby. "I don't have anything from my great-grandmother."

"You want a rosary?"

"You can't give away an heirloom."

"Wanna bet?"

Bria carries the rosary in her hand as the two of them walk down the street to the Boathouse and the big pond that always forms in the summer when the city drops the blast gates at the Wellington Street dam. She lets it swing one way. And then she swings it the other way.

"Is that what Catholics do with rosaries?"

"You're supposed to count the beads one by one," says Bria.

"Why?"

"Who cares." Bria catches the crucifix and turns it over. "See those nine scratches? That's the number of times my great-grandmother was raped by the priest."

"No shit?"

"Who knows," says Bria. "Happened back when dinosaurs ruled the earth."

"This that residential school business?"

"Florence was sent to St. Anne's," says Bria. "To hear my grandmother talk, it was a really crappy place."

"There was a movie on TV about residential schools and stuff like that," says Tabby.

"You watch it?"

"No," says Tabby. "I don't like depressing shit."

When Bria and Tabby get to the Boathouse, they each get an ice cream cone. Bria gets vanilla. Tabby gets butterscotch swirl.

"Kinda exciting week. Aliens land on the moon. The Pope lands in Edmonton."

"My grandmother wants me to fly out there and give the rosary back to the Pope. In person."

"I don't think they'll let you get that close."

"No way I'm going to fly anywhere to give an old rosary to some old white guy," says Bria. "Got better things to do with my time."

"You could mail it to him."

"I'd rather give it to the aliens," says Bria. "How can you eat that stuff?"

"What?"

"Butterscotch," says Bria. "Yuck."

"You should try the stuff they serve at Autumn Leaves."

"How's the job going?"

"It's a job," says Tabby. "You still going to university?"

"Not going to waitress all my life."

Tabby makes a face. "What am I supposed to do when you're off in Ottawa?"

"Kingston."

"Whatever."

Bria's grandmother is waiting for her when she gets back to the house.

"I got peaches," says Bria.

"Did you find anything in your purse?"

"And some of those doughnuts you like."

"I went online," says her grandmother. "There's a late-night flight to Edmonton that you can make. I'll pay for the ticket."

"I'm not going to Edmonton."

"He's giving a speech tomorrow. At the Ermineskin reserve. You could give him the rosary then."

Bria marches to her grandmother's dresser, takes the rosary out of her purse, and puts it back in the cheese box. Then she goes to her room, shuts the door, lies on the bed with her iPad, and watches videos of unusual animal friendships.

That evening, Bria and Tabby go to a concert at Silence on Essex. Gary Diggins and Jeff Bird are on a double bill with the Vertical Squirrels. Afterwards, they walk downtown to the new fast-food place on Macdonell. Bria gets the spring-roll appetizer. Tabby gets a spicy papaya salad. They sit at the tables set up on the sidewalk and watch the cars go by.

"I like it better," says Tabby, "when songs have a melody."

"It's improv," says Bria. "It's not Norah Jones."

Tabby stirs her salad with her fork. "So, what happened with the rosary?"

"Stuck it back in the cheese box."

"Your grandmother's feelings hurt?"

Bria shrugs. "She wanted me to fly to Edmonton tonight."

"We should get something to drink," says Tabby.

"Good idea." Bria stands, opens her purse. Then she sits down with a thud. "Shit."

Tabby gets the drinks. Green tea for her. A Coke for Bria.

"Jeez," says Tabby, after she sits down. "Your grandmother's sneaky."

Bria stares at the rosary on the table. "What the hell," she says. "What the hell."

"She must have put it back in your purse when you weren't looking."

"Yeah, well, enough is enough," says Bria.

"What are you going to do?"

"How can you do that?"

"What?"

"Papaya in a salad?"

Bria and Tabby take the long way home, walk through the park that fronts the river, and stop in the middle of Gow's Bridge.

"It's kind of cool to have an old stone bridge in town," says Tabby. "And a river."

"You see the buoys in the water by the dam?" says Bria.

"The two white things?"

"How far you think that is?"

"No idea."

"Think I can hit them?"

"With what?"

Bria takes the rosary out of her purse, weighs it in her hand.

"You can't do that."

Bria takes a step back, cocks her arm, comes forward and flings the rosary as hard as she can. It sails off in a high tumbling arc into the setting sun and the water.

Tabby starts laughing and shaking her head. "Shit," she says. "You are one bad ass."

WHEN BRIA GETS HOME that night, her mother and father and her grandmother are sitting in the living room, glued to the TV.

"What's up?"

"The Pope," says her father. "He's been attacked."

"They think it might be a terrorist," says her mother.

"Wasn't a terrorist," says Bria's grandmother.

"Quiet," says Bria's father. "There's breaking news."

Sure enough, a large banner appears at the bottom of the screen that says BREAKING NEWS. A solemn-looking guy in a sports shirt stands in front of the camera, holding a microphone. You can see out-of-focus people milling around behind him.

"Behind me," says the man, "you can see law enforcement officials who have moved in to quell the riot."

"There's no riot," says Bria's father, "and I don't see any police."

The scene on the TV changes to a palatial room where an older man in a red outfit is talking to a young woman with a microphone.

"Quiet." Bria's mother raps on the table. "I want to hear this."

"I imagine," the young woman is saying, "that this attack was completely unexpected."

The man in red is tall and heavy-set, with a full head of white hair that hangs around his face like a bright cloud. "Yes, Rosanna," he says, "it was."

"Do you think," says the young woman, "that this attack was in retaliation for the physical and sexual abuse at Native residential schools?"

"The Holy Father is hardly responsible for the past actions of misguided individuals. Such an idea is ludicrous."

"Some have suggested that church policy and practice are responsible."

"Equally ludicrous."

"Then who is responsible?"

"History, of course." The man smiles and straightens his shoulders. "History is responsible."

Bria's father steps closer to the TV. "That's Cardinal What's-his-face. There was an article on him in *Alberta Report*."

"The good news is that the Pope was not badly hurt," says the woman, and she holds the microphone up so the cardinal doesn't have to bend down to answer the question. "It appears that the injury is little more than a scratch."

"Any attack on the Holy Father is an attack on God."

"So, now what will you do?"

"Pray, of course," says the cardinal looking directly into the camera. "We shall pray."

"So," says Bria, "what happened?"

"Somebody threw something at the Pope," says Bria's mother. "Hit him in the face."

Bria's grandmother turns to her. "Now, aren't you sorry you didn't go to Edmonton?"

For the next hour, Bria gets to watch the same footage over and over and over again. The Pope standing on a platform behind a plastic shield. And then, suddenly, his head snaps back, his hand flies to his cheek.

There are a series of clips of the Pope being shoved into a white van and whisked away. Bria can see the blood on his face and on his cassock. It's not a lot of blood, but it's blood nonetheless.

"I'm going to bed," says Bria. "They'll just keep showing the same clips until hell freezes over."

"They'll have new stuff tomorrow," says Bria's father. "Maybe even an arrest."

By the time Bria gets up the next morning, the banner on the TV reads Arrest Imminent. The same man is on the same spot. Someone has muted the sound.

"Tabby called," says Bria's mother. "Said to call her right away."

"There any Cheerios left?"

"The peaches are still a little green," says her mother. "I had to put them in a paper bag."

"I want peaches with my cereal."

"I saved you a half," says Bria's mother. "The Vatican is up in arms."

"Pope gets hit in the face with a rock," says Bria. "I'll bet they're upset."

"Wasn't a rock," says Bria's mother. "It was a rosary."

After breakfast, Bria calls Tabby. Tabby answers on the first ring.

"Did you see the news?"

"Big deal."

"The Pope gets hit in the face with a rosary?" Tabby does a quick *ta-ta*. "A rosary."

Bria holds the phone out, bangs it against the wall. "Hello. Earth to Tabby. Earth to Tabby."

"Think about it," says Tabby. "You throw the rosary away, and the Pope is hit with a rosary."

"Not the same rosary," says Bria.

"Just saying."

"Not the same rosary," says Bria. "End. Of. Story."

"You have to admit it's a big coincidence."

"What are we doing today?"

"Billy Kiddle wants me to have sex with him," says Tabby.

"Darlene's boyfriend? The one who works for the real estate guy?"

"I mean, I'm flattered," says Tabby. "But Billy? Ewww."

BRIA PUTS ON HER jeans and a sweatshirt and heads for the river. She picks up a couple of stones from near the abutment, walks to the middle of Gow's Bridge, throws the first one as hard as she can. Doesn't even come close to the white buoys.

Then she throws the second one. Same result. Then she walks home.

Her grandmother is waiting for her.

"Did you hear?"

"About?"

"The Pope."

"He got hit in the face," says Bria. "Big deal."

"He got hit in the face with a rosary," says her grandmother. "They can't get the bleeding to stop. It's not serious, but they can't get it stopped completely."

"I'm going to go to the mall," says Bria. "I have to get new runners."

"Do you still have my mother's rosary?"

Bria pats her pockets, checks her purse. "Must have left it at Tabby's house," she says.

"Is that right," says Bria's grandmother. "Is that right."

BRIA GOES TO THE mall, finds the place that sells religious items. She's never been in the store before, and she's not keen to be in it now. It smells of candles and incense and other creepy stuff. The woman behind the counter reminds Bria of Beverly Hofstadter from *The Big Bang Theory*.

"Help you?" asks Beverly.

"Rosary," says Bria. "For my grandmother."

"You got here just in time," says Beverly. "We're almost sold out."

"Of rosaries?"

"Normally, we have lots, but after the incident with the Pope . . ."

"People are buying rosaries?"

"Two and three at a time. Some are calling it a miracle."

"Getting hit in the face is a miracle?"

"Others think it's poetic justice."

"I need one that's made out of cedar of Lebanon," says Bria.

"No such luck," says Beverly. "That model was the first to go."

"Great."

"It's going to get worse." Beverly makes a sour face. "Mark my words, it's going to get out of hand fast."

When Bria gets home, she locks herself in her room and goes online to shop for rosaries. She can't believe how many different kinds of rosaries there are. Full custom rosaries, partly custom rosaries, combat rosaries with bullets in place of beads, zircon rosaries, stone rosaries, plastic-bead rosaries in Day-Glo colours.

Most of the rosaries are cheap enough, but Bria finds a diamond and gold model for $10,000 and another with emerald and ruby beads on a platinum chain with a twenty-four-karat gold crucifix for $23,000.

She finds several sites that sell rosaries with wood beads. Some tell you the kind of wood. Some don't. She finally finds a company that sells cedar of Lebanon rosaries, but it's in Jerusalem and the shipping costs are more than the rosary and the delivery time is four to six weeks, and if you want to buy anything, you have to open an account and provide a credit card number.

Which Bria doesn't have.

That's when Bria sees the small print under most of the rosaries that says ITEM ON BACK ORDER.

THE NEXT MORNING, BRIA'S cellphone rings. It's Tabby. She's at the front door.

"Is the TV on?"

"No."

"You have to see this."

Tabby trots into the living room and turns on the set. The BREAKING NEWS banner is back along with a second banner that says LIVE WITH SUSAN RENALDO.

"Renaldo's the one with the microphone," says Tabby. "The guy in the suit is with Vatican security and the other guy is a Jesuit."

Tabby turns up the volume.

"So," says Renaldo, "has there been any progress with the investigation?"

"We have the rosary that was thrown at the Pope," says the security guy, "and we are interviewing several people of interest."

"The Holy Father is resting comfortably," says the Jesuit, "and is recovering from his injuries."

"Which were?" asks Renaldo, as though she doesn't know what they are.

"His cheek was cut," says the Jesuit. "And there have been complications."

"Complications," says Renaldo, as though she doesn't know what they are. "Could you elaborate?"

"It was a large, heavy crucifix," says the security guy.

An insert appears in the top right corner of the TV. It's a close-up of the rosary and the crucifix.

"Doesn't look all that big," says Tabby.

"How many rosaries have you seen?" says Bria.

"Guys always think things are bigger than they actually are," says Tabby.

Renaldo's face fills the screen. "A shocking turn of events," she intones. "The Pope, the leader of the Catholic Church, hit in the face with a rosary. So far, no one has come forward to claim responsibility, but reliable sources have told CBC that authorities are confident that the rosary itself is expected to provide clues as to the attacker's identity."

Tabby points the remote at the set. "Wait for it."

"According to our sources," says Renaldo, "the rosary that was thrown at the Pope is at least fifty years old. But what has officials baffled are the marks on the back of the crucifix."

Tabby shifts from one foot to the other. "Wait for it."

The Jesuit holds the rosary up for the camera, the crucifix laid out flat in his hand.

"This is the crucifix that was thrown at the Pope," says Renaldo, "and as you can see, there are distinctive markings on the back. What do you make of this?"

"You see the marks?" says Tabby.

Bria sees the marks. Four scratches with a diagonal through them and four separate scratches.

"It is our belief," says the Jesuit, "that we are dealing with a disturbed individual."

"We believe the nine scratches represent the number of times he has already assaulted members of the clergy," says the security guy.

"Are the scratches new?"

"No, Susan," says the Jesuit, "they're not."

"Which would indicate a long-standing grudge," says the security guy.

"Might the marks mean something else?" asks Renaldo.

"Serial assault," says the security guy. "This is our working hypothesis."

Renaldo turns to the camera. "There you have it. The Catholic Church under attack. Stay with us as we follow this story and provide you with all the breaking news as it happens."

Tabby hits the mute. "So, what do you think?"

"I think I'm going to have breakfast."

"That's your rosary."

"No, it's not."

"Okay, it's your great-grandmother's rosary," says Tabby. "How many rosaries are going to have scratches like that?"

WHEN BRIA'S GRANDMOTHER COMES home from shopping, Bria comes clean.

"I threw it away. I'm sorry."

"How hard did you throw it?"

"Not hard enough to reach Edmonton."

"Still, it did hit the Pope."

"It didn't hit the Pope," says Bria.

Bria's grandmother thinks about this for a moment. "I suppose," she says, "that it's possible there were other special girls who got special rosaries."

"Sure," says Bria, "the church ran a whole bunch of residential schools. There's probably a shitload of scratched-up rosaries out there."

"Language," says Bria's grandmother. "Language."

THE CUT ON THE Pope's face doesn't heal right away, and the networks quickly field panels of experts who spend a good deal of prime time debating the theological differences between infections and stigmata.

"Infections can be cured," says one authority. "Stigmata cannot."

That storyline is replaced almost immediately by reports of a worldwide epidemic of priests and monsignors being pelted with rosaries, along with several archbishops and a cardinal in Prague.

"What is telling," observes one commentator, "is that in each instance, the rosaries are old, and the crucifixes have distinct markings on the back."

Bria watches the reports to see if anyone is going to explain exactly what it is about the age of the rosaries and the marks that is telling.

"Seems as though my mother wasn't the only one who kept her special rosary," says Bria's grandmother.

"It's copycat mentality," says Bria's father. "You hit one priest with a rosary and, suddenly, everyone wants to hit a priest with a rosary."

"Fox News is blaming the aliens on the moon," says Bria's mother.

"Priests versus aliens," says Bria's father. "That's a cage match I'd watch."

"They stopped the bleeding," says Bria's mother. "Now the cut on the Pope's face just leaks a little from time to time."

Bria thinks about ordering the cedar of Lebanon rosary from Jerusalem. She thinks about scratching nine tics on the back of the crucifix, thinks about slipping the beads into her grandmother's dresser.

But she's guessing that once something like this is out of the box, there's no putting it back.

Jackson Mosley is on the stepladder, patching the holes in the wall that his stepdaughter's boyfriend made when he pulled the drapes down in order to show Darlene just how angry he was.

John or Owen or James is the latest in a long string of deadbeats and moochers.

"He has a job," Darlene tells her stepfather. "You should like that."

So far as Jackson can tell, the only job any of Darlene's boyfriends has ever had is smoking weed and sitting on the sofa playing video games.

"He treats me like a queen," says Darlene.

The curtain rod had been held in place with molly bolts, and when Owen or James or John yanked the drapes down, the bolts tore through the plaster and left small craters in the wall.

"And he's good with Jor-El."

Jackson cringes every time he hears the name. Who the hell does that to a child?

"Jor-El is Superman's father," Darlene explains. "I wish you would stop calling him Button."

Jackson likes Button. Button likes Button.
"Billy thinks Jor-El is a strong name."
Billy? Who the hell is Billy?

THE WALL IS NOT going to be a quick job. Jackson is going to have
to spackle the smaller holes, put screen and drywall mud over the
larger ones.

Spackle and mud.

It's not a hard job. It just takes time. And it's annoying.

Sand and paint with primer.

A job he shouldn't have to do.

Paint and hope the new colour will match with the old. Otherwise, Jackson will have to paint the entire wall, perhaps the entire
room. All this while, Zoltan the slobber hound romps around the
room, wanting to play.

Who the hell names a dog Zoltan?

Jackson has been clear about the pet question. His house, his
rules. And his number one rule is no deadbeat boyfriends and no
dogs. Darlene points out that Zoltan isn't her dog, which isn't the
dog's fault. And Zoltan makes her and Jor-El feel safe.

Jackson doesn't ask if Zoltan makes Darlene feel safe from
James or John or Owen. Or Billy, for that matter. The drapes answer that question.

Along with the garage door.

One of Darlene's chucklenuts tried to drive her car out of the
garage with the garage door closed, and bent the door. It still
works, but there's a crack that runs down the centre, and each time
the door is raised or lowered, there is a grinding sound that tells
Jackson the door isn't going to last much longer.

"Everyone deserves a second chance. And he's a lot better than Donald."

Jackson has forgotten who Donald was, and he suspects that Darlene has, too.

"It's not Billy's fault," Darlene tells her stepfather. "It's the aliens."

EVER SINCE THE SPACESHIP landed on the moon, the aliens are being blamed for everything from power outages to the cost of food, declining church attendance to mortgage rates, baldness to incontinence.

Why not blame Darlene on the aliens as well? It's tempting, but Jackson knows that this is just frustration speaking. Fetal alcohol something or other. Jill has tried to explain it. Alcohol during a pregnancy, the effects it has on the brain of a child, nothing to be done about it.

The house Darlene and Button and Zoltan the slobber hound live in is Jackson's house. A house he bought when he and Ruby were married, before Ruby died, a house he lived in until he and Jill got together.

They didn't need two houses. Jackson didn't want to sell his, and Jill didn't want to sell hers, and neither of them wanted to live with Darlene. So, a spare house for a disabled daughter/stepdaughter with a young son seemed a reasonable solution.

AFTER HE PATCHES AND paints the wall, Jackson will have to waste the better part of a day roaming the ReStore in search of curtain rods and sorting through the junk at Value Village (which no longer has anything to do with value) for a set of curtains.

Of course, the first priority is that the drapes be the right size, that they cover the large living-room window. Maybe he'll be able to find a set that doesn't clash with the walls. But he's not going to lose any sleep over incompatible colours and out-of-date patterns.

If they fit, they fit.

Jill is in the kitchen, stirring something in a pot.

"How'd it go?"

"Fine."

"You didn't yell at her, did you?"

"I never yell at her."

Jill puts her hands on her hips. "Jackson Mosley."

"Her boyfriend made a mess of the wall. Pulled the curtain rods out by the roots."

"His name is Billy."

"Billy? What the hell happened to Owen or John or James?"

Jill gives the pot a stir.

"You should have seen the place. The dog was loose. Dishes in the sink. Piles of clothes all over the house."

"Dirty or clean?"

"Who the hell knows. I don't think Darlene knows. We should sign her up for one of those reality shows. *Slobs Are Us. Happy Hoarders. Landfill, Canada.*"

Jackson pauses to catch his breath.

"And the washing machine doesn't work. I think she burned out the motor stuffing clothes into it."

"Not so loud," says Jill. "You'll wake Jor-El."

"He's here?"

"I told her we would take him. Give her a break."

"So, she gets a free house and a free car and free babysitting, and *she* needs a break?"

"You want to put the plates on the table?"

"I can't keep up, Jill. She's killing me."

"It's just spaghetti. I wasn't up to making much more than that."

"Any dessert?"

THE CALL COMES AS Jackson and Jill are finishing dinner. Jackson doesn't answer the phone anymore. He can't stand listening to Darlene's voice.

"If she wants more money," says Jackson, "tell her to go to hell."

Jill puts a hand over the phone. "It's the police. Darlene is in the hospital."

Jackson sags in the chair.

Jill holds up a hand. The person on the other end of the line is talking. Jill nods, says, "Mm-hmm," nods, says, "Mm-hmm" a few more times.

"Yes, I understand. Yes, we'll come."

Jackson shakes his head, mouths, *No, we won't.*

Jill hangs up the phone, sits back, puts her knife and fork on the plate.

"You need to go to the hospital."

"Car accident?"

"They didn't say."

"I don't want to go to the hospital."

"Someone has to look after Jor-El." Jill crosses her arms, hugs herself. "Besides, you're better at this sort of thing."

"No, I'm not."

"Try to be kind," says Jill. "Try to see her side."

JACKSON FINDS HIS STEPDAUGHTER on a gurney in a corridor along with other patients on gurneys. Her face is bruised and her lip is split. Her eyes are closed, and for a moment, Jackson is tempted to leave her sleep, turn around, and go home.

"Daddy."

Jackson takes a deep breath, looks in his back pocket, finds a smile. "What happened?"

"That's all you want to know?" Darlene's split lip begins to quiver. "You could say you're sorry. You could say you love me."

"I'm sorry. I love you. What happened?"

Darlene sniffs, wipes her nose. "I fell."

What? Out of a plane? This is what Jackson *wants* to say. This is not *what* he says.

"Billy didn't hit me, if that's what you're thinking."

That is exactly what Jackson is thinking.

"How do I look? I look terrible, don't I?" Darlene wipes her nose with the sheet. "I need my cellphone. It's in the bag."

Someone has set a clear plastic bag on top of Darlene's clothes. Jacket. Scarf. Pants. Shoes. Jackson unties the knot. Finds the cellphone.

"I have to call Billy. He'll be worried."

An envelope falls out of the bag. Jackson bends over, picks it up. It's large and yellow. Someone has stamped URGENT. IMMEDIATE ATTENTION across the front in red.

Jiffy Loans on York Street.

Jackson turns his back, opens the envelope, stares at the single sheet of paper that demands a minimum payment of eight hundred dollars. Jackson slumps against the wall, slowly bangs his head on the drywall.

Darlene is assaulting the phone with her thumbs. "I know he's home. He's playing video games. I'm in the hospital, and he's playing video games. I'll bet he's forgotten to feed Zoltan. I can't live like this. Nobody cares about me. I might as well die."

Jackson keeps his mouth shut.

Darlene throws the phone to one side. "I'm going to need money for gas."

"What?"

"I'm almost out of gas."

Jackson holds up the letter. "What's this?"

Darlene frowns. "I don't know?"

"Did you take out a loan with Jiffy Loans?"

"What? No. Why would you even think that?"

"It's addressed to you."

Darlene takes the letter, reads it once, reads it again. "Oh, right," she says.

Jackson waits.

"This is Seth's."

Jackson knows there is no point in asking.

Darlene rolls her eyes. "*He* took out a loan."

"Then why are they asking you for the money?"

"No idea." Darlene picks up the phone, works her thumbs. "Son of a bitch. He's still not answering."

"Why are they asking you for the money?"

"I don't know. God, Daddy, I'm hurt. I'm in pain. You could be sympathetic."

Jackson feels a cold chill run through him. "Did you co-sign the loan?"

"Can you drive over to the house and kick Billy off the sofa? Tell him to get his ass up here?"

Darlene hasn't had a job for over three years. Jackson can't imagine anyone letting her co-sign a loan. She hasn't got any collateral.

"And can you feed the dog?"

Except for the car that he and Jill bought her.

"Did you put your car up as collateral for Sam's loan?"

"Seth," says Darlene. "I guess."

"So, if you don't repay the loan, they're going to take the car."

Darlene's eyes flash. "They can't do that. It's Seth's loan. I was just helping."

"They'll take the car."

Darlene is sobbing now. "They can't do that. It's not fair."

"And where is Seth?"

"What does that matter?"

"If it's Seth's loan, then he needs to repay it."

"Is that all you care about? What about me? If I was abducted by the aliens, you wouldn't give a damn. You'd be happy if they took me."

Jackson folds the letter, puts it in his pocket.

"If you were my real dad, you'd love me."

"I love you." The declaration comes out flat. It's the best Jackson can do.

"It's because I'm white," says Darlene. "You don't love me 'cause I'm white."

Jackson rubs his head. He closes his eyes, rubs his head, counts to twenty.

"Do you think the aliens are fucking with Billy's head?"

"What?"

"He doesn't mean to hurt me. Maybe it's the aliens."

Jackson closes his eyes, counts to twenty. Then he counts to twenty again.

"You and Mom are going to have to look after Jor-El," says Darlene. "Just until I get out of the hospital."

"SHE CO-SIGNED A LOAN?" Jill is watching one of her reality shows. "And put the car up as collateral?"

"It was Seth's loan."

"Who's Seth?"

"She's blaming us and the aliens."

"Keep your voice down, honey. Jor-El is sleeping."

"She wants us to look after him until she gets out of the hospital."

Jill nods. "And we can do that."

"What the hell," says Jackson, "while we're at it, why don't we get her a nanny and a butler?"

"Why are you so angry?"

THE NEXT DAY, JACKSON goes to the house. Darlene is still in the hospital. Jill has taken Button to the park to play on the slide and the swings. The place is empty. No dog. No asshole boyfriend. The patches have dried. Jackson wraps a fresh piece of sandpaper around a block of wood and begins a slow and steady motion, back and forth, back and forth.

Until he's sanded everything down to the studs.

L ate afternoon and Gary Tidy drives to Victoria Glen, parks his car, goes directly to the pro shop. Jimmy DeBartolo is waiting for him.

"Mr. T," says Jimmy D, "ready for that new set of clubs?"

Jimmy D believes in custom-fitted golf clubs the same way a Texan believes in steak. And when he speaks the names of the club makers—Callaway, TaylorMade, Cobra, Titleist, Ping, Cleveland—he does so in tones normally reserved for precious jewels.

Or final-round tickets to the Master's.

"Good with what I got."

"The Wilsons." Jimmy D shakes his head. "Steel shafts? I'll bet they're stiff. Am I right?"

"Chuck Mason foursome," says Gary. "I think we're off in the next twenty."

"You get older and your swing speed drops." Jimmy D takes a seven-iron off the rack, waggles it about. "Could be time to switch to a lightweight graphite shaft and a more forgiving head."

"I'm thinking of quitting golf," says Gary.

"What are you? Twenty-three, twenty-four handicap?" Jimmy D hands Gary the club. "You let me fit you with a custom set, and you'll drop three, four strokes, guaranteed."

Gary has to admit that the club is lighter than his seven-iron, and it does feel good in his hands. The deep-red shaft is an added bonus. Next to green, red is his favourite colour.

"Three to four strokes." Jimmy D takes an imaginary stance, takes an imaginary swing. "Three to four strokes."

CHUCK MASON AND NICO KARRAS are waiting for him by the ball washer. Jackson Mosley is on the putting green.

"Jackson has a new putter," says Chuck. "Fourth one this season."

Gary watches Jackson putt. It doesn't look as though the new putter is going to be any better than the old putter.

"Come on," Chuck shouts at Jackson. "Save the good ones for the course."

THE FIRST HOLE AT the Victoria Glen Golf Club is a par five, 484-yard dogleg to the right. The fairway is wide and flat with four sand traps at the turn, two in front of the dogleg and two across the fairway in the short rough.

Gary knows that if he hooks his ball off the tee, it'll wind up in the parking lot, bouncing off cars. And out of bounds.

He's done that.

Or he can slice it and have the ball land on the driving range. And out of bounds.

He's done that as well.

Straight down the fairway is the best. Big hitters like Chuck can cut the dogleg, fly the first two sand traps, and catch the fairway.

Gary has never been able to fly the dogleg, but the first hole is where he's gotten his greatest number of birdies. He's gotten two eagles as well, has the balls signed and tucked away for safe keeping in his sock drawer.

"Gentlemen,"—Chuck tosses the tee into the air to set the order of play—"start your engines."

Gary gets to go first. Then Chuck, Jackson, and Nico.

"Lead the way," says Jackson. "Don't even think about the driving range."

The first hole is not a difficult hole, and this is the way, Gary believes, a golf game should start. Like life. In a manner most likely to give you a false sense of hope and potential. Indeed, Gary imagines that life is very much like the first hole at Victoria Glen.

Take out your driver, look down the fairway, safe in the knowledge that nothing has gone wrong.

Yet.

"Don't hook it," says Chuck. "And if you do, hit Jackson's car."

Gary puts the ball on the tee, lines himself up with the fairway. So long as he doesn't swing, he can delude himself into thinking that life, like golf, is under his control.

"You waiting for Christmas?" says Chuck.

But Gary isn't about to be rushed. He takes his time. He likes standing on the tee, the breeze in his face, all his illusions shiny and intact.

"This better be worth the wait," says Nico.

The ball leaves the club and flies straight down the fairway, slides past the sand trap, comes to rest in the second cut. It's a long drive, and now Gary has a chance to get to the greens in two.

"What the hell," says Chuck.

"It's the aliens," says Jackson. "They're giving lessons."

"You figure our little green friends are serious about that manifesto?" says Nico.

"It's bogus." Chuck tees his ball. "I heard some kid in California made that damn thing up."

Chuck cuts the corner, as he always does, and is lying in the middle of the fairway with a short iron into the green. Jackson hooks his shot into the rough on the left side. Nico winds up in the trap at the corner.

Gary walks down the fairway with Nico. "How's your mom settling into that retirement place. Sunrise something?"

"Autumn Leaves," says Nico.

"Expensive?"

Gary's ball has a clean lie. With a strong shot and a good roll-out, he might make it to the dance floor.

"My mum's dead, and I have no idea where the old man is," says Gary. "Mind you, if he did show up, I'd sell him to the aliens for parts."

Jackson plays first. He hits a nice shot out of the rough that pulls up about one hundred yards from the hole. Nico hits an eight-iron out of the sand trap and back onto the fairway. Gary tops his second shot, but it skitters through the grass, rolls to about fifty yards from the green.

"Shake it off," says Nico. "Pitch and a putt."

Chuck lands his second shot on the top shelf of the green. Which is going to make for a tricky putt. Jackson puts his third into the thick grass at the back of the green.

"Anybody got a weed whacker?"

The grass is thick and dark green and over Jackson's ankles. Gary isn't sure that Jackson can even see the ball. Gary tries to think of something clever to say, but nothing comes to mind.

"Do what Chuck does," says Nico. "Use your toe wedge."

"Twenty says I stick the green," says Jackson.

"Done," says Chuck.

Gary feels his cellphone vibrate. He doesn't want to look at it. He can guess what the call is about.

"And another twenty says you don't get out of the rough," says Chuck.

Jackson chips the ball onto the green, tries not to look surprised.

"Guess it's true," says Nico. "Even a blind squirrel can find a nut now and then."

Gary's fourth shot gets on the green, but he's left with a short, left/right break for par. This is the pattern to his game. Good shot, bad shot, on the beach, in the pond, good shot, sad shot, bad shot, sad shot.

"At least you're below the hole," says Chuck, who is putting for an eagle.

Jackson pulls his new putter from the bag, strides to the green. "Double or nothing I make the putt," he says. "And I'll throw in my stepdaughter."

"Double or nothing," says Chuck. "And you keep your stepdaughter."

Gary doesn't know how Ellen found out. It isn't a big deal. Just something that happens. An accident. A fender bender. Tripping over a crack in the sidewalk.

"Waiting," says Chuck. "Getting old standing here."

"Danny DeVito," says Jackson.

Gary lines up the tough five-footer, strokes the ball, and watches it slide by the hole on the low side.

"Blame it on the aliens," says Nico.

Chuck misses his eagle putt, has to settle for a birdie. Jackson and Nico par the hole. Gary puts a bogey six on his card.

"Speaking of the aliens," says Chuck as they all walk to the second tee, "did you see what happened in Texas?"

"This about the big blackout?" says Nico.

"Third one in the last four months. Governor is blaming the mess on the aliens and on illegal immigrants running their air conditioners."

"Immigrants even have air conditioning?" says Gary.

Nico is sure that aliens and immigrants have nothing to do with the trouble in Texas, that the electrical blackouts are the fault of the private companies that built cheap, substandard electrical grids, that believe profit comes before service.

"Aliens get blamed for everything," says Jackson.

The second hole at Victoria Glen is a 396-yard, par four, slight dogleg left. The fairway runs downhill to a narrow irrigation ditch that cuts the fairway in half, and then heads back up to an ample green.

Gary is not keen on the second hole at Victoria Glen. Chuck will be able to fly the hazard. Gary will be lucky to catch the down slope and roll out onto the short flat before the ditch. Whatever he does, Gary does not want to slice the ball.

Chuck plays first, easily clears the ditch. "I smell another birdie," he says.

Nico hits his ball to the left and winds up on the side of the hill in the short rough. Jackson uses an iron to split the fairway and come up thirty yards short of the hazard.

"Better safe than sorry," he tells everyone.

Gary tees his ball up, assumes the stance, checks the line, takes a deep breath, and goes through his last-minute checklist.

Head down. Club face square. Make a full swing and follow through. And whatever you do, he tells himself, don't slice.

Don't slice.

Don't slice.

Don't slice.

Chuck stands at the side of the tee, shades his eyes, and follows the flight of the ball. "Going to have fun with that one," he says.

"Keep your elbow in," Nico tells Gary. "You do that, and you'll lose that slice."

"How's your mom liking the rest home?" asks Jackson.

"Fine," says Nico.

"Expensive."

Nico shakes his head and makes a whistling sound with his mouth. "It's a wonder I can afford to play."

"You want expensive," says Chuck, as they walk down the fairway, "try the green fees at Whistling Straits or Pebble Beach, or Shadow Creek in Vegas."

"Winter something," says Jackson, "right?"

"Autumn Leaves," says Nico.

"What do you figure?" says Chuck. "You think the aliens play golf?"

GARY'S BALL IS IN the deep rough to the right, and he's not able to find it right away.

"Don't forget the new rule," says Chuck. "Under 18.2, the time allotted to search for a lost ball has been reduced from five minutes to three."

Nico tries to look sympathetic. "If you can't find it, you'll have to go back to the tee and hit a second with a penalty stroke."

"Stroke and distance," says Chuck.

"Got it," shouts Jackson, and drops his hat to mark the spot.

"That kind of luck," Chuck tells Gary, "you should buy a lottery ticket."

Gary takes his phone out, looks at the screen. There are several nasty emojis in a row. Ellen is angry. Okay, he gets that. And she has said some awful things, things she'll probably want to take back once she's calmed down. The word DIVORCE is in capital letters.

Okay, the affair was a bad idea, a lack of good judgment. But neither Ellen nor Brenda is making his life easier. A workplace affair. They happen all the time. It didn't mean anything. Besides, it was Ellen's fault as much as his. And Brenda's, for that matter.

But he's the one who has to pay the price. He's the one who gets punished. He's the one who will be exposed to public scrutiny. He's the one who might lose his job.

Where's the justice in that?

By the time everyone makes it on the green, Chuck is lying three, Nico and Jackson are both lying four. Gary is lying six. But only because he rattled his second shot off the large willow and wound up in the pond.

"What I don't understand," says Nico as he waits for Chuck and Jackson to mark their balls, "is how the hell are we going to get along with aliens. I mean, we don't even get along with ourselves."

"The new racism," says Jackson.

"It's not racism," says Chuck. "People just like to be with other people who look like them and who have the same values and who speak the same language."

"Community," says Jackson.

"Exactly," says Chuck. "I mean, aliens probably don't even eat the same sorts of things that we eat."

"Hamburgers," says Jackson, "beer, potato chips, pizza, poutine, anything deep-fried."

"Maybe they'll want to eat us," says Nico.

"Gentlemen," says Chuck, lining up his putt, "prepare to be amazed."

THE THIRD HOLE IS 137 yards, par three, straightaway over a pond. Gary hates this hole, or more properly, he is intimidated by the carry over water to a green that is severely sloped back to front. Each time he steps to the tee, he remembers all of his shots that have come up short.

Today, the foursome ahead of them is still on the green.

Chuck leans on his club, grunts. "Who knew that Sly and the Family Stone even played golf."

"Why don't you say it a little louder," says Jackson, "so they can hear you."

"It's a joke," says Chuck. "Christ, you guys got no sense of humour."

Gary tries to remember an all-Black singing group, so he can join in. All he can come up with is the Righteous Brothers.

"Jesus," says Jackson. "The Righteous Brothers are white."

"Closest to the pin?" asks Nico. "Five-buck pool?"

Chuck hits the green. Nico is closer to the pin but off the surface in the short rough. Jackson puts his ball inside Chuck's.

"Lucky ducky," says Chuck. "Ten says you choke."

Gary puts his ball in the water and has to play from the drop zone. His third shot, one plus the penalty, skips onto the green and runs up to within a foot of the hole.

It's small consolation. No matter what he does, the best he can hope for is a bogey.

"Good chip," Jackson tells him. "The drive was crap, but that chip was sweet."

Gary smiles, but he's thinking that he may have to incur an injury that will necessitate his dropping out of the round. A twisted ankle, a wonky rotator cuff, an emergency at the dealership.

Ellen. He could certainly use his wife as an excuse.

Chuck walks to the hole, flips Gary's ball back to him. "That's good," he says. "Hell of a shot."

So, now Gary has a bogey and isn't feeling quite as useless, and maybe the injury or his impending divorce can wait for another hole or two.

CHUCK AND NICO AND Jackson and Gary have to wait again on the fourth tee for the foursome in front of them to clear the fairway.

"You know," says Chuck, "there are courses in the world where you don't ever have to wait."

"Sure," says Jackson. "Private courses for rich white assholes."

"Augusta National," says Chuck. "Liberty National. Cherokee Plantation."

"Wolf Point," says Jackson. "Domaine Laforest in Quebec and Royal Golf Club in Agadir."

Gary doesn't need to play a world-class course. Victoria Glen is enough of an annoyance.

"So, what's this I hear about you and Brenda Price?" Chuck asks.

Gary stands still, stops breathing.

"Shit," says Jackson. "You having an affair?"

Gary chuckles, waves a hand in the air. "Where did you hear that crap?"

"Jesus," says Nico. "Does Ellen know?"

"First rule of having an affair?" says Chuck. "Don't get caught. And if that doesn't work, blame it on the aliens."

THE FOURTH HOLE AT Victoria Glen is a par four, 452-yard, dog-leg right. The fairway slopes down at the turn and runs out to three large sand traps that guard a small green.

Gary hits a serviceable drive, as do the rest of the guys.

"So, just how pissed off is Ellen?" asks Jackson.

"Don't think Gary wants to talk about his wife," says Nico.

"Okay," says Jackson. "Let's talk about hockey."

"You hate hockey," says Nico.

"A bunch of white guys on skates, whacking a black puck around with sticks?" says Jackson. "What's not to like?"

"So, let's talk about hockey," says Chuck.

"Yeah," says Gary, "let's talk about hockey."

BY THE TIME THEY get to the fifth tee, Gary has had it with golf. He's eight over par with a hard stretch of holes ahead. He'll be lucky to break a hundred.

Jackson settles into a rehash of how Canada screwed up its vaccine program. Nico tries to turn the conversation back to the aliens and what to expect once they actually appear in public. Chuck keeps on about hockey and who the Leafs should have picked in last year's draft.

The rest of the holes fly by. Good, bad, embarrassing. Gary tries to concentrate on the verdant fairways, and the pleasant creek that runs through the course, and the fluffy clouds floating in the blue, blue sky.

Chuck gets three birdies in a row.

Jackson sinks a long, twisty putt on the fifteenth.

On the sixteenth, Jackson blasts a ball out of the sand and hits the flag stick.

AS THEY ALL WALK off the eighteenth, Gary adds up his score. Ninety-seven. No, ninety-six. Saints be praised. At least the last game of his lacklustre career stayed in double figures.

Through the window of the pro shop, Gary can see Jimmy D talking to a couple of golfers. He can't hear what they're talking about, but he catches the occasional word.

Nike. Draw biased. Perimeter weighting. Swing speed.

Gary hoists the bag onto his shoulder and heads straight to the car. Without looking back. A biblical moment. Lot on his escape from Sodom and Gomorrah.

"Hey," Chuck shouts to Gary. "If the aliens haven't eaten us, you available next week?"

"Count me out." Gary throws the clubs into the back of his pickup. "I'm quitting golf."

"Yeah," says Nico, "me too."

Jackson shuts his trunk. "So, same time?"

GARY STANDS BY HIMSELF in the parking lot. Brenda is at the dealership. Ellen is at home. Aliens are on the moon.

Gary leans against the side of the car. It's cooler now with a gentle calm that is all too rare. He watches the sun as it settles into the trees, and wonders, not for the first time, if life might be better with a set of fitted clubs.

It takes Thea longer than she expected to walk across town. Her hip slows her down, forces her to take breaks along the way. It would have been nice if the city had put benches along the streets, but they haven't.

Fortunately, there are bus shelters.

Of course, the bus shelter benches are for bus passengers, but Thea doesn't think anyone will mind an old woman with a bad hip sitting quietly, waiting for a bus to arrive that she won't be taking.

The Blue Bird Café is where it has always been. Thea hadn't planned to stop, but she has discovered that all the walking has made her hungry, and since she isn't going to get lunch at Autumn Leaves, she decides to indulge herself on her first day of freedom.

The café looks much the same as it did when she was a regular, and she is able to get a window seat, so she can see the street, watch the people go about their lives.

People who have families who love them, people who have houses rather than rooms in a detention centre.

"Mrs. K. Long time, no see."

Thea can't remember the young woman's name. Annabelle? Amy? Allison?

"We heard you had moved." The badge on the young woman's blouse says Bria. "The retirement place over on Folsom?"

"What's the special?" Thea asks. She was sure the woman's name started with an *A*.

"Meatloaf and mashed potatoes," says Bria. "Wish someone would put me in a retirement home."

"What's your soup?"

"Cream of tomato." Bria takes a pen out of her apron. "Someone else fixing all your meals. Someone else cleaning up."

"I'll take the soup," says Thea. "A dinner roll with butter. And a coffee."

Bria puts a hand on her hip, sighs. "Can only imagine what it's like to sit around and do nothing."

Thea is tempted to give Bria her Autumn Leaves key card, so she can spend a day in Thea's room. To see just how much fun incarceration can be. When she was living on her own, Thea got up when she pleased, went to bed when she was sleepy, ate what she wanted when she wanted. And if she wasn't hungry, she didn't eat until she was.

At Autumn Leaves, all these things are done on someone else's schedule.

Bria is back with the coffee. "You take it black, right?"

Thea is pleased that Bria remembers. "Only way to drink coffee."

"I like a little sugar and cream in mine," says Bria. "Haven't seen your son around much. He used to come here with you."

"He died," says Thea.

"Oh my god," says Bria. "I'm so sorry."

"He wasn't the best of sons," says Thea. "Did you know he tried to sell my house?"

Bria glances back toward the kitchen. "Oh, look," she says, "your soup is up."

The Blue Bird used to make its own soup. But the soup in the bowl in front of Thea is from a can. Thea can tell that as soon as she tries the first spoonful. In fact, it tastes exactly like the soup they serve at Autumn Leaves. The dinner roll is okay. It's soft and warm. The butter melts and soaks into the bread.

Bria comes back with a piece of apple pie. "Everything is on the house," she says. "On account of your son. We're all so very sorry."

Thea hadn't meant to say that, but she's angry with Nico, with the cavalier way he has treated her.

"If there's anything we can do," says Bria, "all you have to do is ask."

Now Thea is going to have to figure out a way to bring Nico back to life. Or find another place to have lunch.

"There was a young man who used to work here," says Thea. "Big and strong. Brian or Benjamin."

"Tim," says Bria.

"Maybe he could help me?" Thea softens her face, the way she does when she wants to make Nico feel guilty. "Would that be possible?"

"Not a problem," says Bria. "We all liked your son."

Thea is amazed at how quickly Tim is able to yank the For Sale sign out of the ground. She wonders if her son would be able to accomplish the same feat with such facility.

Probably. But then, she remembers, he's dead.

"Kinda cool," says Tim. "Your house is listed with my uncle. Chuck Mason? Mason Realty?"

Thea has a key to the house in her fanny pack. She was supposed to give the key to Nico when he moved her to Autumn Leaves. But she didn't.

"Oh dear."

"Something wrong?"

"My fanny pack," says Thea.

She tries to remember the last time she had the pack. At the mall? At the hospital? Did she have it when she got back to Autumn Leaves?

"I don't have my fanny pack."

"Man," says Tim. "That sucks."

The bathroom. She might have left it in the bathroom at the hospital.

"My key was in the fanny pack. Now, I don't have a key to the house."

Tim rocks back on his heels, furrows his brow in a way to suggest that he's thinking. Then his eyes brighten.

"Hey, you see that?"

Thea follows his line of sight, but all she sees is her house locked up tight, the windows dark.

"The lockbox," says Tim.

Thea isn't sure what Tim is talking about, but she likes his hopeful tone.

"Real estate agents use it to store keys. That way, any agent who wants to show a house can just open the box and let themselves in."

Now Thea sees it. "That thing hanging off the handle? There's a key in there?"

"Should be."

"A key to my house?"

"You need a combination to open the box," says Tim. "Good news, Uncle Chuck uses the same combination for all his boxes."

"And you know the combination?"

Tim has the key out in less than a minute, and Thea is through the front door before a second minute goes by.

"If you're moving back," says Tim, "you might consider getting the cylinders changed."

Thea has no idea what he's talking about.

"See, a lot of people have had access to the key to your house. You expect that all the agents are honest, but with so many people coming and going, you're better off to be on the safe side."

"Change the cylinders?"

"It's real easy," says Tim. "That way, you'd have a brand-new key that no one else has. Be a load off my mind, I can tell you that."

"How do I do that?"

"Heck," says Tim, "I can do that for you. Take out the old cylinders and get new keys made."

"I'd like that," says Thea. "My son will pay you for it."

"Isn't your son dead?" Tim pats Thea's hand. "My granny had memory problems too. I still can't believe she's gone."

Tim gets the necessary tools from his car and takes the cylinders out.

"Be back in about an hour," he says. "You settle in and leave everything to me."

"I'll find my chequebook," Thea tells him, even though she has no idea where it is. Or whether the account is still open.

"No worries." Tim gets into his car. "Pay me back next time you come to the café."

The house is dark and cold. But the lights work, and the refrigerator is running and the furniture is still here. Thea guesses that it's because the real estate people want to show the house off at its best.

She checks the freezer in the garage. She's hoping that Nico was too lazy to deal with the frozen food, and she's right. The freezer is full. Mostly frozen dinners that Thea bought whenever they went on sale. Two for one. Half price. Past-due-date reductions.

There are several macaroni and cheese and one of the beef bourguignon. Tonight, she'll be able to eat what she wants when she wants.

Thea sits down on the sofa, turns on the television, and is delighted to find she still has cable.

Maybe Nico isn't lazy after all. Maybe he knew that she could never be happy at Autumn Leaves. Maybe he left her house intact so she could move back in whenever she wanted.

Which is exactly what she has done.

A coma. That's it. Her son was in a deep coma. Car accident, complications from surgery, allergic reaction. As good as dead. An elderly mother confused and in denial.

No, wait, not elderly. Mature.

But now, suddenly, today in fact, he's recovered. A miracle. The sort of thing you see every day on TV. Prayer in action. Maybe the aliens will play a part. Whatever the reason, Bria will be delighted.

So will Tim.

There might even be another free meal to celebrate the resurrection of Nico Karras, and the return of the prodigal son to the bosom of his loving mother.

However, before any of that can happen, Thea has to prepare herself and her house for the assault that is surely to come. Autumn Leaves will have noticed that she has gone missing by now, certainly by this evening. If they're efficient and concerned about a lawsuit, they will call Nico and the police in that order. By the time she finds the nostalgia channel and the *Matlock* reruns, Thea Karras will be a wanted woman.

The idea of being a fugitive delights Thea more than she would have imagined.

Thea doubts that the cops will look for her here, and she hopes that Autumn Leaves will tell the authorities that she's an old woman with memory issues. This will lead the cops to look for her on the streets, lurching about in alleys, stumbling into traffic. And when they don't find her, they will begin searching the woods along the river for her body.

By then, Tim will have changed the locks, and she'll have the only key. Plenty of time to flood the moat and pull up the drawbridge.

Nico might figure it out eventually, but by then it will be too late.

Thea sinks into the sofa. So nice to be home. The place smells the same, and with all the curtains shut, it has the deep comfort of a cave. Maybe the aliens will launch an attack, and then everyone will be too busy to look for one old woman.

The only problem is the Blue Bird Café. If the newspapers pick up the story and publish a picture and a name, Bria or Tim might see it and rat her out.

She'll watch the news. If the story breaks, she'll go back to the café right away. She'll laugh and tell them how the whole thing's a big mistake, how it's been straightened out, how there's no need for concern.

Good.

And, at the same time, she'll tell them about her son's miraculous recovery.

How has she gotten so old so fast? Her mind is fine, but her body isn't keeping up. A well-tuned engine in a wrecking-yard body. She has pictures of herself when she was young and vibrant. When she was sexy. When she had energy and didn't have to squint at the words on a menu. Is she going blind? She can see big things well enough, but now watching TV is a chore. Most times, she closes her eyes and just listens to the dialogue.

And now, as she sits in her own house, she begins to go over her life. Not for the first time. Not for the last. Maybe if she can figure out what she did wrong, she'll be able to go back and correct it. Maybe the aliens have perfected time travel. If you could go back in time whenever you felt like it, it would be better than immortality.

Much better.

If you could control time, Thea realizes, you could pinpoint the best moments of your life and play them over and over again. Stay in an endless loop of happiness.

For instance, the time Thea took eight-year-old Nico to the lake and watched him dive underwater to pick up coloured stones. He brought them to her, arranged them in a pile, a pirate's treasure of precious gems. Later, the two of them, sitting on the rocks, wrapped up in a towel, as the late afternoon wind came up and cooled the shoreline.

And she could avoid the moments of agony. The moments she never talks about. The moments she keeps buried deep inside her.

And what about the dull, grey middle? Thea doesn't know why life is made up of such parts. She just knows that it is.

But now she is back in her house with enough food to last her for the battle ahead. There's no need for her to go out, except maybe to have lunch at the Blue Bird.

No. Bad idea.

That's what they want. For her to abandon her fortress. Nico. The turnkeys at Autumn Leaves. The modern world that has no place for old people. Just waiting for her to walk across the moat and expose her flank.

Not happening.

If frozen macaroni and cheese dinners are the price of freedom, so be it. Here she is, and here she'll stay. No one is going to take her life away from her again.

As for the aliens, well, maybe they're kinder to their parents. Maybe they understand that you can't tell someone how to live their life. And if they don't, well, then they're no better than the rest, and Thea Karras is ready for the lot of them.

Let them come. Let them blunt their swords against the gates. Try to shout the walls down for all she cares, but tonight, at least, they will not pass.

Tomorrow, she'll deal with the missing fanny pack.

The Lunar Drive-in.

Fifteen acres with a 50-by-120-foot screen, a perimeter fence, a ticket booth, and a concrete-block snack shack with a faded sign.

THE LAUNCH PAD.

"Reason it's so cheap," Chuck Mason told Herb when he showed him the property four years ago, "is because the zoning won't allow you to do much else with the land."

Chuck ran a finger across his tablet, showed Herb an article on drive-ins. "They're supposed to be making a comeback."

Herb had walked from the back fence to the screen, the ground rising and falling under his feet like an ocean wave frozen in place.

"Ramps are still here," said Chuck, "but the speaker posts have all been removed. Now, you got an FM transmitter that broadcasts the movie audio to your car radio. And no more dual thirty-five-millimetre film projectors. Everything's digital."

The Launch Pad was musty with the stale memories of popcorn and hot dogs, pizza and soft drinks. Movie posters in the lounge area: *The Incredible Shrinking Woman, Drums Along the Mohawk, The Great Escape, Psycho.* Two pinball machines. *Medieval Madness* and *The Addams Family.*

Herb tried the lights, checked the taps in the bathrooms, flushed the toilets.

"The neon rocket ship sign on the roof?" Chuck flipped the switch. "Darn thing still works. You can't buy stuff like that anymore."

Herb had to agree. The neon sign was certainly a stunner.

"But to be honest, the value's in the land. Couple of years from now and we get a new city council that understands business? Bam! Bam, bam! Zoning gets changed, and you turn all this into condos, a shopping mall. Whatever. Make a fortune. And weekends, while you're waiting, you can rent the space out for one of those swap-meet thingies."

Herb flipped the switch for the neon rocket on and off a couple of times.

Chuck handed him the offer to sign. "We're all sorry about Katherine."

Herb isn't sure how Katherine would have felt about the drive-in. He couldn't imagine he would have done such a thing while she was alive. That was the puzzle of being with another person. Sometimes you change part of who you are in order to facilitate a compromise.

Katherine wanted a large family. Herb didn't want any children.

So, they only had two.

And sometimes, compromise wasn't necessary.

Katherine was fond of European sedans. Mercedes, BMW, Audi. Herb preferred pickup trucks.

So, they bought one of each.

Katherine wanted to travel. Barcelona and Venice, Paris and Prague, Berlin and London. Herb wanted to stay home.

Health settled that question.

Herb moved in the week after the sale closed. He turned the lounge area into a bed-sitting room. Recliner, dresser, flatscreen TV, area rug. He had Fausto Plumbing convert one of the restrooms into a master bath.

"Nothing to it," Fausto told Herb. "We can take out a toilet, use the existing drains. You want a water-saver shower head?"

Herb went with an expensive twelve-inch rain head. So he could stand under a waterfall until the hot water tank went cold.

"You really plan to live here?" Fausto asked him.

It had taken Herb a couple of tries before he figured out the digital projector. But now, he can watch any of the movies that came with the place.

While he hits golf balls.

Each evening, after dinner, Herb turns on the sign, starts a movie, takes his clubs out to the pad of artificial turf that he's put on top of one of the swales, and hits balls into the screen, tries to knock John Wayne off his horse with a six-iron. Uses the driver to catch Clint Eastwood in the crotch with a high fade.

He doesn't bother with the audio, finds that the films are much improved without the soundtrack and the dialogue.

Who could ask for more? The evening laid out soft and silent. The pleasing sound of the club face as it smacks the ball. It's like shooting things, but without the blood and the screaming.

Herb has always been an avid golfer. Club membership. Tournaments. Part of a regular mix-and-match gang. Eighteen holes. Dollar a hole. One tie, all tie. No carry-over. Beer on the patio afterwards. War stories and bad jokes.

The guy who gets a five-iron for his wife.

It used to make Herb laugh.

But after Katherine died, his interest in golf faded. He no longer looked forward to the games, to sitting around on the patio with a beer, reliving well-struck shots and putts that dropped, debating the merits of the new crop of clubs that were more forgiving than the last crop of clubs, balls that were guaranteed to fly farther and straighter.

In spite of all the empirical evidence to the contrary.

He had tried playing golf by himself. In the evenings. When the course was mostly empty. When he could walk the fairways hand in hand with the long shadows, and stand alone on the greens.

A compromise between the social and the solitary. A halfway house. An attempt to rekindle his spirit, reinvigorate his love for the game.

Instead, the twilight rounds stripped away the magic and the mystique, revealed golf for what it really is. A protracted walk with periodic pauses and bathroom stops. A way to pass the time without having to do anything that might make the world a better place.

Much like buying a defunct drive-in and spending what is left of a life hitting balls against a screen.

Herb knows that he didn't have to buy a drive-in in order to practise the pantheon of shots that golfers need to master. But after Katherine died, he discovered that, while he still likes hitting golf balls, he doesn't like other people.

And here at the Lunar Drive-in, he can be alone.

Herb is able to get the Launch Pad fitted for satellite internet and cable TV. That's a plus. The lounge area is small, but it's all the space he needs, all the space a man in his twilight years can reasonably expect.

Get up, eat breakfast, hit balls, have a nap, eat lunch, watch the golf channel to see if they have any new tips on how to clip a short-sided ball onto the green with a sixty-degree wedge, hit some more balls, eat dinner, a movie on the big screen, hit more balls.

A simple, solitary life. A life that's winding down. A life that has lost its forward momentum and is beginning that long drift and slow fall.

Been here long enough.

Words to live by.

Herb has begun to look at the best-before dates on various products. Milk, eggs, fish. Sometimes, it's hard to find the dates, and he suspects that the companies are not keen for the public to have this information.

Fair enough.

But how would it be if people had expiry dates? Wouldn't that be fun? Everyone comparing dates. Why does she have a better date than me? Who does she think she is?

Ever since he started thinking about this, he can't buy cottage cheese without wondering about the woman standing in front of the freezer, looking at the ice cream. Is her expiry date better than his? Will he outlive her?

Does anyone really care?

Sure, we care. We just can't do much to change the time we have. Herb figures that he's already past his date, is on borrowed time. If he checks, will he find a half-price sticker on his forehead?

Which is why he bought the drive-in. To have a place of his own, where he can find a splinter of quiet happiness. A place where he can die in peace.

Dead with a three-wood in his hand.

It sounds like a refrain from a rockabilly song.

> *Dead with a three-wood in his hand*
> *Not the way I had it planned*
> *Here is where I make my stand*
> *Dead with a three-wood in my hand.*

Vocals by Buddy Holly, Patsy Cline, or maybe Johnny Cash. Except they're all dead.

Like Katherine.

How does he want to die? Of course, he's thought about it, hopes that death is not a professional golf tournament. Four days of tramping over rolling fairways, climbing in and out of sand traps, avoiding water hazards and deep rough.

He hopes death is quick. Like a tee shot. One moment, the ball is sitting on the little wood peg, at peace, in perfect balance with the world.

The next, it's not.

On Monday, Herb stands in the early evening light, tees up a ball. On the big screen, the 7th Cavalry rides into a large encampment of Cheyenne and Lakota on the Little Bighorn River.

He makes a slow, leisurely swing, and the ball explodes off the club, the strike a little low and a bit on the toe. But the driver has built-in forgiveness, is biased for a draw, and the ball flies straight, catches Dustin Hoffman in the side of the head.

Herb hears it before he sees it. The sound of a car slowing down. A utility van, in fact. A utility van that pulls off the road, heads for the gate, rolls past the ticket booth and into the drive-in without slowing down.

Herb has been meaning to shut and lock the gate. The van keeps coming, parks at the side of the Launch Pad. Herb ignores it, drives a ball into a knot of soldiers hunkered down on a rise overlooking the river, watches as several of the men pitch forward in the prairie grass.

"Hello."

A woman gets out of the van. Tall, with a marshmallow face. Not as old as Herb, but old nonetheless. And a tight young man in a suit that is one size too small.

"Mr. Good Runner?"

Herb tees up another ball.

The woman takes a card out of her briefcase, holds it out. The card is dark blue with gold lettering.

Terram Primum.

"I'm AIC Marcia Campton, agent in charge for the Northern District."

Herb turns the card over. There's a phone number on the back, along with an email address.

"And this is AIT Wayne Rice. He's one of our agents in training."

Rice points his chin at the screen. "Is that John Ford's *She Wore a Yellow Ribbon*?"

"No," says Campton. "It's Arthur Penn's *Little Big Man*."

On the screen, the big battle scene is in full swing. Herb tries to decide between the nine-iron and the pitching wedge. Settles on the nine-iron.

Campton pulls her hair away from her face, tucks it behind her ear. "Is there someplace we can sit down and talk?"

Herb doesn't want to sit down. He doesn't want to talk. He wants to watch the movie. He wants to hit balls. He wants to be left alone.

"And something to drink," says Campton. "Something to drink would be welcome."

Nathaniel and Abigail.

Herb remembers the care he and Katherine had taken with the names of their children. But by the time the two were teenagers, the names had been shortened to Nate and Abby, cut in half by other children who had no inkling how much work went into coming up with the names in the first place.

Wrong names, as it turned out.

Nathaniel should have been Leo or Bruce or Lance.

Abigail should have been Holly or Sally or Lucy.

But how can you know these things? There you are in the hospital and the nurse hands you a form. Where would be the harm in just calling the baby "Baby" and waiting a couple of years until a good name came along all on its own?

CAMPTON AND AGENT-IN-TRAINING RICE sit on the sofa in the Launch Pad. Soft drinks in cans. Herb doesn't want to delay their departure. They can take the cans with them when they go.

"Terram Primum is an NGO based out of Calgary." Campton pauses, waits. "Good Runner is a Blackfoot name, is it not?"

Herb isn't about to add any oxygen to the fire.

"Kainai, if I'm not mistaken." Campton smiles, pleased with herself. "Standoff?"

Rice slides a folder across the table. "Perhaps you've heard of us."

There's a large red stamp across the face of the folder that says TOP SECRET.

"Terram Primum is Latin for 'Earth First.'" Campton opens the folder, spreads the pages out. "As you know, aliens have landed on the moon."

"But we don't expect that they will stay there," says Rice. "In fact, there is evidence that a scout ship has already landed on earth."

"Near Standoff, as it happens." Campton waits for a reaction.

Campton looks to be a practical woman. Herb's wife was a practical woman as well. Sitting in the Launch Pad with Campton reminds Herb how much he misses Katherine.

Even though he can't remember her as clearly as he once could.

"Of course, we hope that they will be friendly," says Campton, "but we need to be prepared for any eventuality."

"We need to be proactive," says Rice.

Herb blames the memory problem on old age and the passage of time. The colours of life. Bright and vibrant in the beginning. And then fading until there is nothing left but vague shapes in the distance.

"Drive-in theatres are a key component in that preparation."

Agent-in-Training Rice reminds Herb of Sheldon from *The Big Bang Theory*. If Sheldon were to wear a suit. If Sheldon were to wear glasses.

"What AIT Rice is trying to say is that drive-in theatres could well be our internet to the heavens."

Rice crosses his legs, pushes his glasses up his nose. "What is shown on drive-in theatre screens could be what the aliens will see."

"And what we want them to see," says Campton, "is that Canada is strong and resolute."

Rice taps the stapled pages. "The first two pages list the movies that have TP approval. The second two pages list the films that are discouraged."

Herb leans over, looks at the lists.

War of the Worlds. Approved.

Planet of the Apes. Discouraged.

Rocky. Approved.

Dr. Strangelove. Discouraged.

Top Gun. Approved.

Duck Soup. Discouraged.

Herb finds *Little Big Man*. It's on the second page of the discouraged list.

"The aim," says Rice, "is to show the aliens that we are not to be underestimated."

Herb wonders if Terram Primum should include documentaries on the concentration camps at Auschwitz and Dachau, the Wounded Knee Massacre, the Rwandan genocide, along with shorts on the civil rights movement, Kent State, École Polytechnique in Montreal.

The January 6 insurrection in Washington, D.C.

To demonstrate the full range of human capabilities.

"In addition," says Campton, "we'd like you to keep your rocket sign turned off."

Herb understands that AIC-for-the-Northern-District Marcia Campton isn't asking. However, he has no intention of turning the sign off. He likes the illusion of the spaceship soaring into the heavens, likes the promise it holds for a new beginning, the possibility of a second chance for humankind in a galaxy far, far away.

"A rocket might be seen as aggressive," says Rice. "The aliens could get the wrong idea."

More than anything, the neon rocket with its flashing colours and streaking lights reminds Herb of the Christmas tree Katherine always insisted on having in the house over the holidays. But now that he thinks about *that*, he remembers the arguments the two of them had over the wisdom of killing a perfectly good tree in the service of an irrational myth.

And the memory of the lights and the tree and holding Katherine while the Three Tenors sang "Silent Night" on the TV makes him sad.

Campton clears her throat. "One of the ideas our organization has under consideration is having all the drive-ins around the world show the same film at the same time."

"A demonstration of solidarity," says Rice. "We're thinking *Independence Day*."

Herb hasn't talked to either of his children for a few years now. When Katherine was alive, she made it a point to call Nathaniel and Abigail at least once a week to see how they were doing, to hear their voices, to listen to them complain about life as adults.

Sometimes Herb would listen in on the extension. Sometimes he wouldn't.

Katherine didn't seem to mind that the kids never called her. With two exceptions. Mother's Day and her birthday. The family tradition was that if one or the other of the children didn't call on those days, they were out of the will.

January and May. Katherine's birthday and Mother's Day.

When she died, Herb wasn't sure what to do about that year and the will. In the end, he did nothing, waited to see if the kids would carry on the tradition. Call him on Father's Day and on his birthday.

Hello. How are you doing? Love you. You're in the will.

But they didn't. There had been a moment when he thought he might call them to tell them that they were out of the will for the year, but it seemed petty, seemed unfair to penalize them for something that was someone else's need.

Then again.

THE AGENTS FROM TP leave more cards on the counter, thank Herb for his co-operation, take their soft drinks with them, get back in their van, and drive away.

Been here long enough.

Now that he thinks about it, the smart boys and girls at TP are wrong. *Independence Day* would be a bad choice to show the aliens. Better to show them something funny. Bugs Bunny. Coyote and the Road Runner. Maybe *The Simpsons*.

Better still, a feel-good movie. *Sleepless in Seattle* or *Legally Blonde*. Maybe *Barbie*. Maybe not.

Something they can relate to, something that might make the aliens smile. Or laugh. If they do such things.

Muppets from Space. Perfect.

Herb goes to the main panel, throws the switch, turns the sign on. The rocket ship blasts off, and the drive-in explodes in light. The moon is full in the night sky. From here he can see the lunar landscape of dead volcanoes, craters, and lava flows in vague shades of grey.

But he can't see the aliens, and contrary to the prevailing paranoia, Herb doesn't believe the aliens can see him either.

So, what the hell. Maybe the earth will be invaded tomorrow. Or maybe it won't. Maybe he'll call Nathaniel and Abigail. Just in case.

Hello.

How are you?

Did I tell you I bought a drive-in?

No problem. I can call back later.

HERB WALKS OUT TO the ticket booth, loops a chain around the gate, and locks it. Something he should have done a long time ago. First the woman from the retirement community and now the folks from Terram Primum. Solitude isn't worth much if people can come and go as they please.

Though to be fair, Darby Dock was his fault.

Yes, she backed into his pickup in the Zehrs parking lot. And yes, he let her drive him home. And that should have been the end of it. Except it wasn't. He didn't remember inviting her to the drive-in, but the next evening, there she was with leftover macaroni and cheese and apple pie.

They watched a movie, hit a few golf balls. Herb couldn't say he didn't enjoy the attention, the company. But when she came back two nights later, Herb could see that things could get out of hand quickly.

The chain on the gate should be message enough. Better than a long, painful face-to-face explanation.

HERB GOES BACK TO the tee box, sets a ball on the turf, takes out his nine-iron.

Men in Black.

Why didn't he think of this sooner? The perfect movie for aliens to watch. When he gets back to the Launch Pad, he'll check to see whether it made either of the lists.

Approved. Discouraged. Hard to tell.

Been here long enough.

That's what Herb tells himself as he checks his grip, sets up to the ball.

Swing through. Rotate the forearms. Close the club face. And don't forget to follow through.

Yes, he should call the kids. Tell them they'll always be in the will. Even if they don't call. Offer to go out for a visit. Katherine would like that.

The drive-in sits silent against a black sky. Herb could start another movie, but what would be the point? The aliens don't need no stinking movie. He doesn't need no stinking movie.

There in the darkness, under the sparkle glow of the neon rocket, he finds just enough pleasure breathing in the night air and hitting balls against an empty screen.

Darby Dock sits in her office at Autumn Leaves and tries to log in to her Amazon account.

We have detected unusual activity and have temporarily locked your account. Please contact customer service for further assistance.

This is the same message that Darby has gotten for the past three months. Each time she tries to access her account. Today, yesterday, the day before that, and the day before that, down, down, down through the dusty corridors of time.

She would love to be able to talk to customer service, except there is no Amazon customer service phone number, and the only way Darby can get to Amazon customer service is to log in to her account, which she can't do because her account is locked.

There *is* a phone number for Amazon customer service on the internet, but the number is nothing but a scam.

So, each morning, when Darby gets to work, she tries to log in to her Amazon account, and each morning she gets the "account locked" message. This is the definition of insanity. Doing the same thing over and over and expecting a different result.

Darby points the remote at the flatscreen on the wall, mutes the sound before the woman in a dark-blue business suit and the older man in a sports jacket and tie can tell her everything the world already knows about the aliens on the moon.

Aliens, aliens, aliens, and more aliens.

The world is falling apart, and all these idiots can find to talk about are aliens on the moon.

What about the threat of climate change? Or the bonehead politician and his sexual assault trial? The invasion of Ukraine? The never-ending war in the Middle East? How about a traffic report? Weather for the week?

Professional advice on how to cope with the rising costs of running a retirement home?

Oh, no, not when there are aliens on the moon.

Darby sorts through the bills on her desk.

Holy fuck, holy fuck, holy fuck.

That much for apples? Okay, fresh fruit is out. And maybe they could institute three pasta nights instead of two. Canned soup? Sure. You can still get that on sale. And really, what's the difference between orange juice and fruit punch?

The corporation that owns Autumn Leaves doesn't like any spike in expenses. They prefer spikes in profits. Rack 'em and stack 'em. That's the motto. Squeeze as many soon-to-be-corpses into as small a space as possible with as few staff as the law will allow.

And let them eat cake.

So long as the cake is cheap. And on sale.

Darby tries Amazon again.

We have detected unusual activity and have temporarily locked your account. Please contact customer service for further assistance.

Maybe the aliens can call Amazon for her, explain the situation, threaten to death-ray headquarters if they don't fix the problem.

Darby finds the bill for cable service. Last month, the corporation that owns Autumn Leaves suggested cancelling Netflix and BritBox.

Imbeciles.

Downton Abbey and *Bridgerton* reruns are the only thing that keeps the peace. Does the board of directors want a full-scale prison riot on their hands?

Do they care?

As Darby sits and stares at the computer screen, she's reminded of Frost's lament about having nothing to look forward to with hope and nothing to look back upon with pride, and she wonders if the poet was thinking of Autumn Leaves when he wrote the poem.

Or Amazon.

If Darby's account wasn't locked, she'd be able to return the Kindle she bought from the merchandise megaglop. She had had high hopes for the device, but as with so many other things in her life, it's proven a disappointment. Not the same as a book. Not the same ambience. Not the same feel.

Sure, she can load any number of titles onto the Kindle, and while this is convenient and handy, there are unexpected startles. Many of the novels that she would like to read cost as much as the actual book. And while many others are free or cost pennies on the dollar, they are seldom worth the effort.

A disturbing number have turned out to be soft-core porn.

Most annoying of all, the device, with its greasy plastic cover, has started to smell like the floor around a toilet. Having put up with a husband and a brother, she certainly recognizes that particular stink.

And speaking of her brother . . .

Darby checks her email, and yes, there are several messages from Richard about his ongoing need for a cellphone.

Again.

Darby whacks her forehead. A little too hard. She wants to remind him that he is living in her condo in Victoria rent free, that she pays the utilities and condo fees, but she knows that Richard the mooch, Richard the unemployed, Richard the Lord of La-La Land is immune to reality.

Which is one of the reasons she has decided to sell the place. She can no longer afford her brother *and* the condo. Selling relieves herself of both at the same time. The other reason to dump the unit is the fear that the aliens on the moon will weaken an already weak real estate market.

It will be a nasty surprise for Richard, but Darby has had enough. Between her brother and her ex-husband and the world at large, Darby Dock has had enough, and enough is enough. She has a moment of pleasure as she tries to imagine Richard's reaction when he discovers that his rent-free world is on the block. With any luck, her ex-husband will call with news of a terminal disease.

That would make her week.

We have detected unusual activity and have temporarily locked your account. Please contact customer service for further assistance.

Darby doesn't understand why there isn't an Amazon customer service phone number. What kind of corporation doesn't want to talk to its customers?

Amazon, evidently.

It should be an easy matter to resolve. A call to customer service, an explanation, some security questions, a password or two, and someone somewhere in the known world flips a switch, and all is well.

But in order to contact customer service, Darby first has to be able to log in to her account, and she can't do that because the FUCKING THING IS LOCKED.

Now she sounds like her husband.

Correction. Ex-husband.

Chuck Mason. The real estate maggot. Chuck of the bad temper. Chuck of the wandering dick. Two of the many reasons Darby left him, retrieved her maiden name, blocked him on Facebook.

Chuck went ballistic about the name change. Told her that she couldn't turn back time, couldn't erase history. Made up an analogy about branding cattle that he thought was clever.

"Morning, boss." The woman in the doorway is tall, pipe-cleaner thin, with hair that has been dyed too many times. "A couple of items for your amusement."

Ellen Tidy. Activity coordinator. Darby is sure that she isn't going to like any of the items and that she will not be amused.

"The bus broke down again. Got the residents to the mall on Saturday in good order, but then it wouldn't start. I called Gary."

"And?"

"He said it could be the battery or the starter motor," says Ellen. "But he's not really a mechanic. He just looks after the parts desk."

"The bus is still in the mall parking lot?"

"It is," says Ellen. "We had to bring everyone home in taxis."

Taxis? Jesus. More expenses? What's wrong with a refreshing walk?

"While back on the ranch, Mrs. Franklin isn't any better. Since we no longer have full-time certified medical on staff, we probably need to take her back to the hospital."

Corporate cost-cutting measures. Full-time doctor replaced with a once-a-week rotating doctor. Full-time nurse replaced with a twice-a-week rotating nurse. A defibrillator that no one knows how to use. Three first-aid kits from the Vietnam War.

"And Mr. Trump died last night."

Darby smiles. Finally. Jonathan Trump was nothing but trouble. Demented. Disruptive. Disgusting. Goodbye, Johnny. Good luck.

"Funeral home is picking up the body as we speak."

Darby leans back, allows her body to relax.

"And we have Mrs. Payne," says Ellen. "Again."

Darby moans.

"Seems she saw a special on Fox News about sugar and sugar substitutes and wants us to check the ingredients in the oatmeal."

Joan Payne. A credit to her name. *It's Fox News, Mrs. Payne. Consider the source.*

"I looked," says Ellen. "Three grams of fat, twenty-seven grams of carbohydrate, five grams of protein, zero sugar. No sugar. No sugar substitutes."

Ellen shifts from one foot to the other. She doesn't look nervous, but neither does she look comfortable.

"Something else?"

"Mrs. Karras." Ellen sighs for effect. "She went to the mall with that new girl and the Saturday group."

"What new girl?"

"Tabby What's-her-name," says Ellen. "You know. Your ex-husband's niece?"

"She was in charge?"

"She was."

Darby waits. Not the first time one of the old cows has wandered away from the herd.

"Mrs. Payne was with her. She thinks Mrs. Karras was abducted by the aliens."

Darby is surprised at how calm she feels. "Find Karras. Fire Tabby. Increase Payne's anxiety medication."

"Don't think she's on medication."

Darby puts both hands on the desk and presses down until her fingers begin to turn white. "Must I do everything?"

DARBY MEETS KIKI SANBORN at the Boathouse for lunch.

"I got us a table by the window," Kiki tells her. "We can see the water."

Darby glances at the menu board. Today's soup is chicken gumbo. It's not a favourite. She much prefers the roasted red pepper with sausage.

"So, I heard from Owen," says Kiki. "He's in Key West. It's where conservatives go to buy Cuban cigars."

Darby takes her phone out, checks the messages, puts it on the table by the salt and pepper.

"Problems at work?"

Darby smiles, tilts her head as though someone has given her a gentle slap. "They never stop."

"You'd think that looking after a bunch of old people would be an easy gig," says Kiki. "Falls, sure. A couple of heart attacks. But you got medical personnel to deal with that sort of stuff."

Darby's phone begins vibrating. She watches it as it shakes its way to the edge of the table.

"One of your secret lovers?" says Kiki.

Darby looks at the number on the screen. Victoria. Dick with his daily whine.

"You know I'm your best friend," says Kiki, "so you can tell me anything."

"You don't want to know about my love life."

Kiki nods her head furiously. "Yes, I do."

Darby is glad she hasn't mentioned Herb. Kiki wouldn't stop until she had wrung out every detail.

Of which there are none.

He isn't a lover. He isn't anything. At least not yet. And maybe never.

She ran into the man at the supermarket. Literally. Backed into his pickup, bent the fender in against the tire so the truck couldn't move. Had to call a tow, take it to a body shop.

Darby insisted that she drive him home. The least she could do. Drive him home.

Except home happened to be an old drive-in theatre. Darby was initially put off by the man's living situation. She found the place somewhat creepy but also eccentric, and by the time she left, she began thinking that maybe, at this point in her life, a little eccentric might not be a bad thing.

"You're not getting back with your ex?"

Darby gags on her gumbo.

"But you still think about him."

"Every time I don't have to clean around the toilet or fish the empty condom wrappers out of his pocket."

"Nobody keeps an empty condom wrapper." Kiki makes a fish face. "And reconciliations are happening a lot lately. I think the aliens have made people reassess their decisions. Look at Rory McIlroy."

Darby has no idea who Rory McIlroy is, and she isn't going to ask.

"But then there's Kim Kardashian and Kris Humphries."

The evening after the accident, Darby drove out to the Lunar Drive-in with mac and cheese and apple pie that was left over from Canadian night at Autumn Leaves.

"They were together for seventy-two days?" Kiki rolls her eyes. "Tell me that's not suspicious."

There was a movie playing, a western of sorts. Herb was hitting balls against the screen. The neon rocket was lit. The evening air was alive with the pungent smell of wild mustard from the field across the road.

They talked about the truck, about life. They ate, drank coffee and Orange Crush. Herb showed her how to grip a golf club. By the time Darby got back in her car and drove away, she was damp with the morning dew of romance.

Kiki signals the server. "We are so going to get the scone with clotted cream and raspberry jam."

Back at the office, Darby tries to log in to her Amazon account once again. There's no point. She understands this. But it's become somewhat of a ritual, and if she's honest with herself, being rejected again and again brings with it a certain sexual tension.

Amazon. Herb.

Herb. Amazon.

Not that Herb has rejected her. The two times she's gone to the drive-in, freshly washed and fluffed, with leftovers from Autumn Leaves, he has seemed pleased to see her. Well, maybe not pleased. With Herb, it's hard to tell the difference between pleased and curious, surprised and annoyed.

She's not sure she'd choose to live in a drive-in, though she has to admit that the snack-bar living quarters do have a playful ambience. The sofa next to the popcorn machine. The bed next to the soda dispenser. The old movie posters on the walls, and the bathroom with its shower and four toilets.

The rotary phone on the wall.

Then there's the golf. Okay, she's a good sport. She let him show her how to hold a club, how to line up the shot, how to make the swing. Would she rather be dining by candlelight at La Queen or Petros on the Park? Sure. Could hitting golf balls be the basis of a long-term relationship? Probably not.

But who doesn't want a neon rocket on their roof?

Darby looks up as Ellen comes into her office. The woman has been crying. Her eyes are puffy. Her nose is running. She has her arms wrapped around herself for comfort.

"Tomorrow," says Ellen. "I won't be in tomorrow."

Darby doesn't ask what's wrong. It appears to be too late for that question. So, she waits.

"Personal matter," says Ellen. "I'm sorry."

Darby waits some more.

"I don't want to talk about it."

"Okay."

"And Mrs. Karras is still missing."

"Have we called the police?"

"Not yet."

"The family?"

Ellen shakes her head. As she does, a big dollop of something disturbing falls out of her nose.

"And the bus?"

That evening, Darby puts a RealItalian frozen pizza in the oven and opens a bottle of Peller Family merlot. *Jack Ryan* is on Amazon Prime, but she can't watch it because Amazon has frozen her account, so she has to settle for *Poirot*. It's an episode she's seen before, but she enjoys David Suchet and his nuanced rendering of Agatha Christie's little detective.

She debates going to the drive-in. Herb will have a movie up on the big screen. He'll have the golf clubs all laid out, the balls waiting in a bucket next to the strip of Astroturf. But she isn't in the mood for popcorn and golf balls. And she isn't in the mood for watching sweaty men on sweaty horses chase sweaty Indians across a John Ford landscape.

As she waits for the pizza to cook, she recognizes what she has always known. Herb and the drive-in aren't going to be a happy-ever-after. More a friends-with-benefits sort of thing.

If that.

Darby told Herb about her problem with Amazon, and Herb told her that he didn't have an Amazon account. Darby couldn't believe it. To have an Amazon account that is locked is one thing. To not have an account at all is quite another.

Does the man know it's the twenty-first century?

Darby wonders if Chuck knows how to get her account unlocked. Probably not. Her ex-husband's way of dealing with things that don't work is to yell at them. He shouts at recorded messages when the only person who can hear him is himself.

Maybe what she needs is a vacation. Go somewhere that doesn't have phone service or an internet connection. Someplace where she can forget about Amazon and her blocked account. The Gobi Desert in Mongolia might be nice. A winter getaway in Tierra del Fuego.

After dinner, Darby goes on the internet to discover, once again, that her Amazon account is still locked.

Okay, so after *Poirot*, it's *Castle* reruns and *Storage Wars*.

The next morning, as Darby is getting ready to go to work, the doorbell rings. If her account wasn't frozen, she might have ordered a doorbell camera, so she could see who was standing on her front porch.

It's a young guy in a suit. Backpack. Blue lanyard around his neck. Smiling. Good teeth. Darby can see him clearly through the glass. No idea who he is, and she's not about to open her door to a stranger, even one with good teeth.

The man holds up the identification card hanging off the end of the lanyard.

AMAZON CUSTOMER SERVICE.

Darby waves the young man away. Does it look like her head zips up the back? She knows a scam when she sees one.

But the young man doesn't move. He smiles, presses the identification card against the glass so Darby can read it without getting her glasses.

JONATHAN LUSTIG. AMAZON CUSTOMER SERVICE.

Darby holds up one finger to let Lustig know that she needs a moment, and then she goes to the kitchen and calls the police.

"You've reached police services. Due to higher-than-normal call volume . . ."

Darby can't believe it. She hangs up, checks the number, dials it again.

"You've reached police . . ."

What the hell? What if this was an emergency? What if Jonathan Lustig was a burglar or a rapist or a serial killer?

She dials the number a third time and listens to the entire message, which has a long preamble and a caution that inappropriate or abusive language will not be tolerated. And then she is offered a number of options.

"Press one if you wish to know our location and hours of operation. Press two for traffic court. Press three to be connected to the domestic abuse hotline. Press four to be connected to the suicide hotline."

Darby can't believe it. What about five, to report a crime? Or six, to report an assault in progress? What if Jonathan Lustig tries to break in? What if he needs to be restrained? What if he needs to be shot?

What's she supposed to do? Go on Amazon and order an American with a gun?

Which she can't do, even if she wanted to, because her FUCKING ACCOUNT IS TEMPORARILY LOCKED.

Darby takes a deep breath. OMG. She really is starting to sound like her ex-husband.

Jonathan Lustig from Amazon customer service is still at the door, and he's still smiling. Okay, so maybe he's not a serial killer. Maybe he actually is from Amazon. He doesn't look like a scam, though these days, you never know.

Darby opens the door a crack, keeps herself ready to slam it shut, throw the deadbolt.

"You say you're from Amazon."

"I am. Customer service."

"And you're here about my account? The one that is temporarily locked?"

Lustig takes out his phone and consults the screen. "Darby Dock, 49 Mary Street?"

Darby waits.

"A couple of security questions," says Lustig. "The name of your first cat?"

Darby tells him.

"And your first car?"

Darby tells him that, too.

"Perfect," says Lustig. "That concludes the security check-in."

"So, now you'll unlock my account?"

"Might we sit down?" says Lustig. "I've been on my feet all morning."

Darby thinks about calling Herb. Ask him to come over. Ask him to bring a golf club. Not a driver. Maybe a five-iron. Something with heft. Just in case.

Lustig looks around the living room and the kitchen the way Chuck does when he's listing a house.

"Mid-century builder," says Lustig. "My parents had one similar to this."

"Would you like a coffee?"

Darby has no idea why she offers. She doesn't want Lustig in her house. She doesn't want to make him a coffee.

"That would be lovely." Lustig reads her mind. "But I imagine you're suspicious. You're wondering why Amazon would send someone to a customer's home."

Darby puts cookies on a plate, along with some grapes.

"It's a pilot project," says Lustig. "Selected cities in North America. Amazon wants to see if talking to people in person will increase customer satisfaction and market share."

Darby makes Lustig an espresso. She makes herself an espresso as well.

"If I may ask," says Lustig, "what brand is your espresso machine?"

Darby smiles. She's proud of her machine. She did a fair deal of research before she bought it. She's pleased that Lustig recognizes quality.

"It's a Rocket Cellini."

"Italian?"

"I believe so."

Lustig takes out his tablet and strokes the screen. "Amazon," he says, "sells a great many espresso machines."

He turns the tablet around so Darby can see the screen. "Breville, De'Longhi, Oster, Philips, Wacaco, Chefman. We carry all the major brands."

Darby scans the page. "You don't carry Rocket."

Lustig smiles. "That's because it's not an Amazon-approved brand."

Darby comes to the defence of her espresso machine. "It was top-rated. I've had it for twelve years."

"Oh my god." Lustig makes a gurgling sound deep in his throat, as though he's drowning. "Oh my god."

"I expect to keep it for another twelve."

"And that," says Lustig, "is the problem with your account. That is why it has been locked."

"My espresso machine?" Darby leans back in the chair. "I thought the problem was 'suspicious activity.'"

"Not quite," says Lustig. "In your case, it's suspicious *inactivity*."

Darby waits.

"Your browsing history is quite adequate," says Lustig. "Before we locked your account, you spent a good deal of time looking at all sorts of products. Cellphones, patio tables and umbrellas, non-stick cookware, doorbell cameras."

Darby waits some more.

"But you didn't buy anything." Lustig makes a disappointed emoji face. "In spite of all the reminders that we sent about the items you left in your cart."

"What's wrong with looking?"

Lustig nods. "And while your inactivity is a problem, there is, fortunately, a solution."

Darby has been patient long enough. "Mr. Lustig, I think you should leave."

Lustig smiles. "You still think this is a scam."

"Yes," says Darby, "I do."

Lustig takes out his cellphone, races his thumbs across the tiny keyboard.

"All right," he says. "Try logging on to your Amazon account now."

WHEN DARBY GETS TO the office that day, the police are waiting for her.

"Good morning, ma'am. I'm Constable Virone, and this is my partner, Constable Souto."

Constable Virone is a compact woman with a pleasant face.

"You reported a missing person."

Constable Souto is thin. He reminds Darby of the riders in the Tour de France.

Constable Virone consults her phone. "A Mrs. Carsis?"

"Karras," says Darby. "She's one of our residents."

"Here at the old folks' home."

"Retirement community."

"And she's been missing for . . . ?"

"She disappeared on Saturday," says Darby. "There was a group that went to the mall. She didn't return with them."

"Is there any history of mental illness?"

Darby has already looked at Mrs. Karras's file. "No Alzheimer's, no dementia."

"And there's no reason to believe she was kidnapped?"

"Kidnapped?" Darby hadn't even considered that. "Why would she have been kidnapped?"

"Been an epidemic ever since the aliens landed on the moon," says Constable Souto. "You wouldn't believe the number of people who swear they've been kidnapped by aliens."

Darby waits for Souto to chuckle. "You're kidding."

"You wouldn't believe the calls." Officer Souto holds out his phone. "This is a photograph that your office sent us. Is that a good likeness?"

Darby can't remember what Mrs. Karras looks like. There are more than ninety residents at Autumn Leaves. She doesn't know them all. She doesn't want to know them all.

"Yes, that's Mrs. Karras."

Virone nods. "We'll go to the mall, show her photo to the merchants, see if anyone remembers her. And we'll canvas the area around the mall as well. An old woman on foot can't get very far. Probably find her at a bus stop. Or in the park."

"Thank you."

"Does she have family?"

"She does," says Darby. "A son."

"And he's been notified?"

Shit. That's what she was going to do.

"Yes," says Darby. "And he's very concerned."

"Leave it with us," says Souto. "We'll find her. One way or the other."

DARBY MEETS KIKI FOR lunch at the Boathouse. The soup today is roasted red pepper, and both women order a bowl, along with a scone.

"There's a monthly quota?"

"Not a quota," says Darby. "An expectation."

Kiki finishes her soup and puts the bowl to one side. "And this is actually spelled out in the Amazon agreement you have to click on when you open an account?"

"It's implied. Evidently, capitalism operates on expectations." Darby takes out a pen and draws an upward slanting line on the paper napkin that comes with the scone. "This is the corporate profit model."

"Let me get this straight," says Kiki. "Your account was locked because you didn't meet Amazon expectations?"

"Exactly."

"And in order to get it unlocked, you have to buy stuff?"

Darby cuts off a piece of scone and spreads it with whipped cream. "The Amazon guy suggested that I replace my espresso machine."

"Is it broken?"

"It's twelve years old." Darby puts a lump of strawberry jam on the cream. "According to Amazon, major appliances should be replaced every two to three years."

"So, Amazon has unlocked your account?"

"On a trial basis."

"Well," says Kiki, "at least now you know what you have to do."

"Yes," says Darby. "Now I know."

THAT EVENING, DARBY GOES out to the drive-in, is surprised to find the place locked up, the front gate chained and padlocked. In the distance, the snack bar is dark, the movie screen blank. If Herb is wandering the property with his golf clubs, she can't see him.

She sits in the car, looks at the rocket set against the night sky. Without its neon glow, it's just a grey silhouette. She debates leaving the leftover Swiss steak and mashed potatoes at the ticket kiosk.

In case Herb comes back and is hungry.

But having decided that there is no future for her in old movies and golf, she leaves the box of food on the seat. She can put it all in her freezer for a later meal.

A rotary phone? That should have been her clue.

ON THE WEEKEND, DARBY browses Amazon's website and orders a wristwatch, an electric toothbrush, a set of noise-cancelling headphones, and a jump rope.

On Sunday, she binge-watches her favourite shows on Amazon Prime until her eyes ache.

On Monday, she'll send everything back for a full refund. In the drop-down menu where it asks her for the reason she's returning the items, she'll choose "other" and type in "Alien invasion."

And she'll do this next month and the month after that and after that. She'll do this always and forever, to the end of time.

Darlene sits on the edge of the gurney and swings her legs back and forth. They're pretty good legs, a little thick at the ankles, but with nicely formed calves. She wishes her legs were longer. Like Bria's or Tabby's.

Not that Billy appreciates her legs. He's a tits-and-ass man. That's what he tells her. Tits and ass. Okay, so her ass is bigger than she'd like, and her tits have nipples that stick out like the nipples on baby bottles. She expected that Billy would like her nipples, but he says they're gross. Worse, there are stray hairs that grow around the areolas that she plucks as soon as they appear.

Sure as hell doesn't want Billy or anyone else to see them.

The doctor who examined her was worse than her stepfather. Questions, questions, questions. "How did you sustain your injuries?" "Did someone hit you?" "Do you want to talk to the police?"

Is she crazy? Talk to the police? They'll help for sure.

Darlene just wants to get out of the hospital. Maybe she'll just walk out the door. Would they arrest her if they caught her trying to leave? For sure they'd call her mom, and her mom would tell her stepfather, and she would get yet another lecture from Muhammad Ali.

Aliens. If they catch her, she'll blame the aliens.

She swings her legs some more and notices a corn on her little toe. Where the hell did that come from? It looks like the pimples she used to get on her chin. Fucking gross. She should show it to Billy. Watch him gag.

Not that Billy is Mr. Perfect. He's starting to go bald. She can see the open spaces on his head. And he has a dick the size of a swizzle stick. Nothing like the dicks she's seen on the pornos that Billy watches. They're impressive, but what can you do with a dick the size of a baseball bat besides wave it around?

Billy should have come to the hospital to pick her up, to tell her that he's sorry for hitting her. Even if getting hit was partly her fault. She understands that. She made him angry.

She tries Billy once more. *Answer the phone, or we're done.* The call goes straight to message.

Christ.

Okay. She's going to have to walk home. It's not a short walk. And most of it is uphill. How is that fair?

Darlene gets off the gurney, goes to the bathroom, locks the door. Maybe she'll stay here. Sit on the toilet until she dies. See how Billy and her mother and her stepfather like that. See if they think that's fair.

The purse is on the floor next to the sink. Darlene leans over, picks it up, and now she sees it's not exactly a purse. It's something you wear around your waist. Her mother used to have one.

A fanny pack. That's what it's called. A fanny pack.

Darlene unzips the main pocket. There's a cluster of cards held together with a rubber band.

Thea Karras.

That's the name on the social insurance card, on the health card, on a library card, on an expired Costco card, on a blue hospital card.

There's also a bunch of photographs in a plastic insert. Family photos. Everyone looks happy. Darlene doesn't have any photos of Jackson and her mom. Doesn't have any photos of the three of them. If she did, they wouldn't look happy.

She has photos of Billy on her cellphone, but she's going to erase them as soon as she gets home.

In a second pocket, Darlene finds a fold of cash held together with a paper clip. Two hundred and sixty-five dollars. She counts it twice, just to be sure. The money feels comfortable in her hand. It feels as though it wants to be there. Like a cat curled up on her lap.

There is a picture of Thea Karras on the health card. Born January 20, 1947. Darlene does the math. Eighty-seven. The woman is eighty-seven. Holy hell. Thea Karras is older than her mother. Older than Jackson. She doesn't know anyone who is *that* old.

She'll take the fanny pack to the nurse's station, leave it there. The hospital will have a record of Thea Karras, will be able to get her stuff back to her. Last year, Darlene lost her health card, so she knows what a hassle it is to get a replacement.

She suspects that Billy sold it, even though he swears he didn't.

Darlene puts the cards and the photographs back in the fanny pack. Which leaves the money. What if she kept enough of Thea Karras's money to pay for a taxi? She could leave a note in the fanny pack with her phone number. An IOU to pay the money back.

A loan.

Once Thea Karras knows the circumstances, Darlene is sure the woman will understand.

If she's still alive.

It hits Darlene in the face like an airbag. No one comes to a hospital if they're well. They come because they're sick. And Thea Karras is old enough to be very sick. She's old enough to be dead. And if she is dead, she doesn't need the money.

Certainly not as much as Darlene.

Darlene is considering mortality and Thea Karras's money when there is a knock on the door.

Shit.

"*Ocupado*." Darlene has had a year of high school Spanish, and as soon as she says *ocupado*, she realizes that it should be *ocupada*.

But she has a bigger problem than gender agreement. If Darlene leaves the fanny pack in the bathroom, the person who comes in right after her is probably going to find it and turn it in. And if Thea Karras is still alive, she'll see that the money is missing and call the police, and the police will start an investigation.

There's only one solution. Darlene stands up, flushes the toilet, runs the water for show, clips the fanny pack around her waist, and walks out of the bathroom as though she owns the world.

THE TAXI DROPS DARLENE off in front of the house. She doesn't see her stepfather's truck in the driveway. She's hoping that Billy hasn't returned. She'd like to stash the fanny pack in the closet or under the bed before he sees it. He'll want to take the credit cards, maybe try to sell the health card. The guy is basically a crook. Her stepfather is right about him.

Darlene doesn't know why she hasn't seen this sooner.

The house is empty. Except for Zoltan, who jumps all over her the minute she comes through the door.

"Okay, I'll feed you."

Darlene can smell that something isn't right. Sure enough, the dog has pooped in the corner of the kitchen. This is because Billy hasn't let him out. Well, it's his dog. He can clean up the mess.

The house is quiet, and for the first time in a long time, Darlene feels a peace descend on her. Maybe living alone wouldn't be so bad. Maybe she doesn't need a man to complete her. Maybe she can complete herself.

Except that would mean getting a job.

She doesn't mind working. She doesn't mind making money. It's the available jobs that she doesn't like. Last year, she went to a job fair at the West End Community Centre. A lot of the jobs that were available required a university degree. Which Darlene doesn't have. The ones she qualified for were all entry-level, minimum-wage, dead-end jobs for losers.

Like Billy.

What's the point in wasting your time in a job like that? She needs to find something that isn't boring, something that doesn't involve hot grills and deep fryers. Something indoors with air conditioning.

She's heard about jobs that come with a car and an expense account, jobs that involve travel. That's the kind of job that she wants.

So, Tiger Woods is wrong. She *does* have ambition.

Darlene goes to the refrigerator. Someone has stocked it with fresh fruit and ground beef, eggs and vegetables. Her stepfather. Why doesn't he listen to her? Frozen dinners. If he's going to buy her food, buy frozen dinners.

Fresh stuff goes bad if you don't cook it right away, and cooking is not something she likes to do. Or Jackson could just give her money, so she could eat out. KFC. Wendy's. A&W. Subway. Why waste the time with fresh stuff you have to cook when you can just walk into a McDonald's and come away with a Happy Meal.

Best of all, it doesn't cost any more than making it yourself.

OMG. When did she last eat? With all this talk about food, Darlene realizes that she hasn't eaten since . . . ?

Ten dollars on the taxi. Which leaves $255. Her gas tank is almost empty, so she should put at least twenty into it. And weed. She'll need weed. Forty dollars for that. The good news is that she can get gas and weed at the same convenience store. All of which will still leave her with $195. Plenty left over for a burger combo.

The fanny pack.

Darlene doesn't know why she didn't think of this sooner. If Thea Karras is still alive, the old woman will probably give Darlene a reward for the return of her fanny pack with the cards and photographs.

I found this at the hospital. I think it's yours.

Oh, thank you, thank you. Let me give you a reward.

You don't have to do that.

I insist.

Okay.

Only Darlene doesn't know where Thea Karras lives. She takes everything out of the fanny pack again, and there it is. The blue hospital card. The blue hospital card with the woman's name and address.

Perfect.

But first she needs to get something to eat. Maybe she'll scramble a couple of eggs. Toast with fresh fruit. Maybe take a selfie with the food and send it to her mom to show to Jackson.

After that, she'll gas up her car, buy the weed she needs to help her sleep. Tomorrow, she'll drive over to Thea Karras's house, return the woman's stuff, and collect her reward.

Ellen Tidy.

Spring. The weather unseasonably warm. York Road shut down for repairs. The fifth year in a row. The scandal involving the mayor and the automated speed cameras has replaced the aliens on the moon.

Ellen walks home from Autumn Leaves. Gary's new truck is parked at the curb. The one with the snowplow on the front end. The truck Gary plans to use to clear winter driveways, if winter ever comes around again.

She loads the tailgate spreader with salt, sets the flow control gate, removes the deflectors.

She slides in behind the wheel, checks her makeup, touches the rosary that hangs from the rear-view mirror. Then she starts the truck, raises the blade of the plow, drives to the Walmart on the edge of town, parks at the far end of the lot.

Brenda Price.

The woman called her at work. Wanted her to know. Didn't want to go behind her back. Didn't want to be the second woman. Wanted to be upfront and transparent.

Wanted to meet for coffee at Walmart.

Sure.

Coffee with Brenda the slut.

Ellen watches the people go in and out of the big-box store. Mothers with children. Old women making their way with walkers. Young men in jeans and T-shirts.

Walmart is having a sale on golf balls. The kind that Gary likes. She'll pick up a box or two, maybe find something nice for Brenda as well.

Ellen pulls the truck into gear, drives past the rows of cars, up onto the sidewalk, pushes her way into the store, ripping the double doors off their hinges. Rumbles past the greeter dressed up like a holiday elf.

And stops.

Ellen isn't sure what she's looking at. And then she sees the banner and the large placards announcing Walmart's Summer Christmas Week.

Summer Christmas Week?

Evidently, someone at corporate decided that if one Christmas is good, two are better. Why wait for December? What's wrong with Christmas *deux* in June? Holiday songs are playing over the loudspeakers, urging peace and goodwill. Vendors in the aisles offer free samples of salt, fat, and sugar to anyone with fingers and a mouth. Decorations are hanging from the metal rafters.

Shopping Is Good.

Welcome, Aliens.

Ellen rolls forward, and in this make-believe manger of specials and discounts, in this palace of packaging, in this paradise of many aisles, she turns left.

Turns left and drops the plow blade.

Ellen drops the plow blade and drives down the centre aisle.

Slowly. Careful to avoid the shoppers and the guy on the motorized scooter. The edge of the blade cuts through the side displays, sheering off bags of gummy bears and neon worms, smashing through men's casual wear and women's purses, ripping up tiles as it digs into the floor.

Until she reaches the food section and has to decide which way to turn.

Golf balls. Where would they have golf balls?

Which way to the coffee shop?

She turns right, away from the fresh produce and into frozen foods. Down aisle one, up aisle two, ripping the doors off the freezers, sending ice cream, frozen dinners, and pizzas in brightly coloured boxes flying.

Probably in sports.

Down aisle five. Ellen and her plow blade snick through the dark-green and amber bottles. Olive oil, canola, sesame, peanut. Until the floor is an enormous smear of slick. And, as she tries to make a hard turn, she slides off into pallets of bottled water, side-swipes stacks of countertop microwaves, and crushes a bin of maximum absorbency pull-ups for men.

At first, the shoppers scatter and scream. Scream at Ellen and her sliding truck, scream at their children, scream for someone to do something. But Ellen calmly steers into the skid, engages the spreader, uses the spray of salt for traction, performs a four-wheel drift into aisle six, and methodically destroys the stockpiles of Pepsi and Coke.

And then.

Slowly.

As the crowd realizes that Ellen means them no harm, their mood changes. Excitement replaces fear. A few of the braver consumers begin following the truck. Soon, the rest of the shoppers fall in, shuffling along behind, laying hands on the tailgate, whispering words of encouragement, singing out targets for Ellen to hit.

Candy.

Air fresheners.

Anything with a rollback happy face.

Everyone has a cellphone out now, taking selfies, taking videos for Facebook, tweeting friends to get down to the store right away. Some even push selected merchandise into the path of the blade—shampoo, sugar, bleach—just to see it all explode against the plow. Up and down the rows Ellen goes, laying waste to the glut of Christmas-in-the-summer consumables.

Ellen and the truck rumble into the sports department and take out a long row of fishing rods and reels. But no golf balls.

She charges through the toy section, scattering Barbies, basketballs. Maybe Brenda would like a boxed set of My Little Pony.

And on to the entertainment section. Everywhere she looks, chaos. Everywhere she turns, destruction.

Coffee shop. Where the fuck is the coffee shop?

Until she's managed a complete circuit of the store and is back at the checkout stations with their long, killing chutes of impulse-buy trinkets. Candy and gum, tabloids and phone cards.

Inexpensive treats that even the poor can afford.

And just as Ellen is deciding what to destroy next, just as she's trying to decide what else she can put to the blade, the police arrive.

THE FOUR POLICE OFFICERS arrange themselves at angles to the truck. They shout for her to turn off the engine, to put her hands on the steering wheel. Instead, Ellen turns on the radio and cranks up the volume.

John Fogerty.

Everyone waits. Two minutes. Five minutes. Eight minutes.

Ellen in the Walmart Summer Christmas extravaganza. Ellen in the truck, her foot on the clutch. The officers, their guns out now, their arms aching from having to hold a ready firing position.

Ten minutes, thirteen.

The shoppers continue to arrive and gather behind the truck.

"Get back," the police tell the people.

"Clear the area."

"Move into home decor."

But the shoppers stand their ground. They hold up cellphones, so they can share this moment with friends, so they're ready in case something exciting happens.

And then the truck moves forward. Just a little. And the police move with it, keeping the proper distance, maintaining an effective shooting resolution.

"Stop the truck," they yell. "Stop the truck right now."

Inside the truck, John Fogerty is singing "Fortunate Son." Outside the truck, the police are shouting. Shouting at Ellen and the truck. Shouting at the shoppers. Shouting at one another.

Where in the hell are the golf balls?

Where the fuck is Brenda Price?

What does she look like?

And then the pickup backfires.

Everyone is startled. One of the policemen backs into a display of Skittles and goes down hard in front of the truck. Ellen sees the falling policeman and slams on the brakes. The crowd, which has been following too closely, lurches into the back of the pickup and cry out, just as the engine backfires once again.

And in that moment, the police, come hot from hell, let slip the dogs of war.

A summer Christmas miracle.

When the police stop shooting, no one is dead. Two people wounded. One of the officers hit by a ricochet. An older man grazed just above the knee.

The shoppers slowly find their feet and their courage. Dazed. Cautious. Enraged. They press against the pickup with their bodies, hammer at the sides and fenders with their voices.

Muslim.

Black.

Terrorist.

Alien.

Even though what they find when they force the door open is a blond woman in a Christian truck.

More police arrive and quickly wrap the store in yellow tape.

Ambulances.

Fire engines.

News vans.

Ellen and the truck are hauled away. Bullet holes are discovered along the back walls. Department managers and cashiers hurry between the registers and the parking lot with reports of damage and rumours of looting. The stink of gunfire drifts through the aisles like fog. An instrumental arrangement of "Joy to the World" plays over the store's sound system.

And, then, once again, in the palace of plenty, all is calm. All is bright.

Billy drags the bags of garbage out to the driveway, tosses them into the dumpster. The crap you find in rentals. Rotting food in the freezer. Dead mice in the basement. A bucket filled with old diapers.

Sometimes, he gets lucky. A couple of beers in the fridge. A pack of smokes behind a bed. A shirt in the closet that someone forgot. In one rental, he found twenty dollars in an envelope. There was a card with the money.

Happy birthday, honey. Love, Mom.

That was sweet.

Then there are the things people leave behind that he can sell. A barbecue. Barbells. A toaster. Three chairs. A table. A beat-to-shit sander. Music CDs. Haul them over to the Fergus flea market of a weekend.

Cleaning rentals is not the job Billy would like to have, but working for Chuck is better than sweating over hot grills and deep fat fryers. And it beats breaking into cars, pickpocketing purses at the supermarket, and shoplifting.

Six months in jail for shoplifting? First offence. Okay, first time he got caught. But six months? What the hell is that? This isn't Russia.

Billy throws a skateboard in the back of the pickup, along with the stereo and the speakers. Fifteen for the board, fifty for the sound system. The best find so far has been a gun. About six months back. In a box under the sink. Not a real gun. A starter's pistol. Along with a box of blanks.

The great thing about the gun is that it doesn't look like a starter's pistol. It looks like a real gun. If Billy decided to rob a convenience store, the pistol would come in handy. And it's small, so he can stick it in a pocket, carry it around.

Someone tries to mess with Billy Kiddle, out comes the gun. Billy the Kid. Bang, you're dead.

First time he showed it to Darlene, he fired off a couple rounds. As a joke. Louder than he thought. Zoltan went apeshit, barking and pissing himself. Startled Jor-El, and Darlene went all bananas, started screaming about not wanting a gun in the house, not wanting a gun around her kid.

"It's not a real gun, bitch." And that got her screaming even harder.

Darlene does a lot of screaming for someone who gets everything handed to her on a platter. And now, she's in the hospital. She's going to blame him for that, and yes, he did hit her, but it was mostly her fault.

If she thinks he's going to apologize, she's got another think coming. Probably expects him to go to the hospital to see how she's doing, take her home, but he doesn't have the keys to her car, and he sure as hell isn't going to bounce for a taxi.

She's the one who gets an allowance. A fucking allowance. She can pay for her own taxi.

Maybe he won't go back to the house for a couple of days. Show her what life is like without him.

BILLY TOSSES ANOTHER BAG in the dumpster just as Chuck pulls up in his fancy sports car. An Audi A5 Cabriolet. That's the kind of car Billy wants, although right now, he would take any car. Right now, he has to beg Darlene to use hers.

Darlene who gets everything from her parents. A house to live in, a car, an allowance.

Who the fuck gets an allowance?

And what does she do? Nothing. So far as Billy can see, Darlene doesn't deserve any of it.

Chuck stands at the curb, looks at the dumpster. "The place clean?"

"Almost done," says Billy. "Real mess."

"That's what you say about all the rentals."

"Well, it is."

"Painters are coming tomorrow. Everything needs to be out before they get here."

Billy doesn't like the way Chuck treats him. Just because the guy drives a nice car doesn't mean he's anything special. Probably shit his pants if Billy showed him the gun.

"Not going to need you next week." Chuck hitches his pants. "Probably not the week after either."

"I need to eat, you know."

"When you finish, drop the pickup off back at the house. And I'll need my cellphone back as well."

"Come on," Billy whines. "What am I supposed to do without wheels and a phone?"

Chuck shrugs. "You know where you can find sympathy?"

Billy's heard the joke before. It's not funny. Chuck's not funny.

"It's the aliens," says Chuck. "Rentals are dead in the water. Houses aren't selling. Everyone is sitting on their asses waiting for the aliens to fart."

Billy's tired of everyone blaming everything on the aliens. Darlene has already tried this with him.

Smoking too much weed? It's the aliens.

Not feeling like having sex? Aliens.

Messed up period? Aliens, aliens, aliens.

Hey, how would Darlene like it if Billy smacked her around a bit and blamed it on the aliens?

"Only three ways to make money in this world." Chuck winks at Billy. "Inherit it or steal it."

Okay, so he lost his temper, but that was her fault. Nothing to do with the weirdos from space.

"And there's nothing to say you can't do both."

No need for her to have called the cops. No need for her to have gone to emergency. Should tell Darlene where she can find sympathy.

"What's the third?"

"Real estate," says Chuck.

CHUCK IS FULL OF advice. Most of it is shit. Chuck likes to go on about how the rich don't steal from the rich. They steal from the poor, 'cause there are more poor, and if you're poor, you can't do much about it. The poor steal from each other 'cause they can't steal from the rich.

Blah, blah, blah.

Lot Chuck knows.

"Everyone wants real estate," says Chuck. "Rich and poor. You find a rich person, and they're going to have two, three, four houses at least. Poor person has to rent. It's all real estate. It's all money."

Chuck likes to pretend that he's poor. He leases the Audi. Blah, blah, blah. The bank owns his house. Blah, blah, blah. Taxes are too high. Blah, blah. Chuck is always complaining about money. But maybe that's what rich people do.

Complain.

Inherit money, steal money, real estate. Not much of a choice. The money fairy isn't going to drive up in a Brinks truck, and Billy can't afford the down payment on a garden shed.

Which leaves number two.

Billy has thought about this. Problem is most people pay for everything with credit cards or debit cards. If you're looking for cash, you have to go to a bank. But he's smart enough to know that that kind of shit isn't going to make him rich. It will just land him in jail.

He's thought about getting a safety vest and a clipboard, walking through upscale neighbourhoods looking all official, ringing a bunch of doorbells, and if no one answers, trying the door to see if any are open.

And then what? Grab a couple of cellphones? Run off down the street with a flatscreen tucked under your arm?

You want to steal, the smart play is health cards. He got decent money for Darlene's. And passports. He knows a guy who will buy everything he can bring him. But that shit is hard to come by.

If he had a computer and a printer, he could make up Aboriginal status cards. He saw a story on CBC News about phony status cards. How a single card can sell for up to a thousand dollars.

Maybe that's what the aliens who landed on the Blackfoot reserve out in Alberta are doing. Making up status cards.

Which is when Billy remembers the crazy old guy at the Lunar Drive-in. He's Indian of some sort or another. Hank, Harry. Something like that. Good something. Good Runner.

Yeah. Good Runner. Herb Good Runner.

If Billy were Indian, he'd want a better name than Good Runner. Red Hawk or Screaming Eagle or Iron Bear.

Chuck has talked about Good Runner. Dude buys a drive-in.

Lives in the snack shack. Hits golf balls against the big screen. A real nutcase.

But if the guy is Indian, he probably has a status card, and Billy could use a thousand dollars, especially now that Chuck is going to stiff him on work and take away the truck and the cellphone. Maybe the old fart keeps a bunch of cash lying around.

Indians probably still use cash.

Billy hopes that Darlene isn't home yet. If she's still at the hospital, it will give him a chance to slip in, grab his pistol. Leave a note for her.

I love you.

Don't forget to feed the dog.

Maybe when Billy finishes the rental, he'll drive out to the Lunar. Soon as it gets dark, he'll sneak in. Catch the old guy unawares. Show him the gun. See what pops.

The more Billy thinks about it, the more he likes the idea. The drive-in's isolated, so that's a plus. The old guy is hardly going to put up a fight, and Billy's watched enough MMA to know what he's doing.

Maybe he scores a status card. Maybe he scores cash. Even if the old guy doesn't have a status card, he's sure to have a health card and probably a passport. All rich guys have passports. You don't buy a drive-in unless you're rich.

Cleanup's done. Last items into the dumpster are several boxes of empty wine bottles and a small mattress that smells of dog piss.

Fuck.

Chuck's too cheap to buy him a pair of gloves, so now his hands are going to smell of dog piss.

Billy puts the key back in the lockbox. Darlene is always going on about fairness. At least she has a phone. At least she has a house. And her parents give her money for doing fuck-all. Billy doesn't have a phone or a house, and he doesn't get anything from anyone.

How is that fair?

When he goes to the drive-in tonight, he'll ask the old Indian. See if he can come up with a good answer.

S udi is in the yard, looking up at the eaves of the house.

"The carpenter bees have returned."

A few years back, Nico noticed holes in the cedar fascia and discovered an infestation of carpenter bees. Not only were they chewing long tunnels in the structure of the house itself, but when they were done chewing, they'd hang their butts out of the holes and shit all over the windows.

Brown sticky crap that had to be scraped off with a razor blade.

Both he and Sudi enjoy nature. Ants, moths, flies, mosquitoes. Live and let live. However, after several seasons of chewing and shitting, they've decided to make an exception with carpenter bees.

Yes, in terms of aggressiveness, the bees are reasonably mellow. The males just fly around, dum-de-dum, making a godawful din. The females are somewhat more aggressive, and of the two, only the females have stingers.

Nico looks at the window until his neck hurts. "Who knows not where a bee doth wear his sting?"

"Shakespeare?" Sudi groans.

"*The Taming of the Shrew.*" Nico taps the side of his head. "Act 2, scene 1. Petruchio and Katherine."

"In the play, it's a wasp," says Sudi, "not a bee."

"Close enough."

"And it's a really dumb play."

"'The play's the thing.'"

"How about you stop with the erudition and scrape the bee shit off the windows."

"I'll put it on my list."

Nico tried an exterminator, paid a goodly amount of money for him to spray poison all over the house, and by the end of that week, there were dead birds in the garden.

And the bees were still chewing and shitting.

There was an article on the internet that advised against killing the bees. They're a minor annoyance, the writer intoned, but not overly destructive. Whoever wrote that piece of drivel hasn't seen the house. The bees were bad enough, but while they were busy boring holes and crapping, a rattle of woodpeckers came in behind them and began banging larger holes in the wood to get at the bees and the larvae.

Oceana arrives in the early afternoon with a large, scruffy guy and a large, scruffy dog in tow.

"Hey, sis." Oceana gives Sudi a perfunctory hug, a couple of air kisses.

"So," says Sudi, "it's Oceana now."

"Nope," says Oceana. "It's Cleopatra now. Queen of the Nile."

Nico has a little snort.

"And this," says newly minted Cleopatra, "is Anthony."

"Anthony and Cleopatra," says Sudi. "The world's greatest lovers."

Cleopatra turns to Anthony. "See, I told you she would understand."

"Anthony." The man holds out an enormous paw. "Pleased to meet you."

The dog presses in, leans against Nico's thigh.

"And this is Captain Kirk," says Cleopatra. "He's an Airedale terrier. They hardly shed, and they're more intelligent than most people."

Both the man and the dog look as though they came from the same shelter.

"He's still a puppy," says Cleopatra. "He'll get a lot bigger."

Anthony is tall and thick, covered in hair. Full head. Full beard. A bear in bear clothing.

Captain Kirk wanders over to the Subaru and raises a leg.

"No," Anthony snaps. "Bad dog."

He startles Captain Kirk, who leaves a trail of puppy urine down the side of the tire.

"He's not quite housebroken yet," says Cleopatra. "But he's a sweetheart."

Cleopatra has dyed her hair once again, and the new colour and the old colours are beginning to merge into a soft clay grey.

With flame-red tips.

"Anthony is an olfactionist," says Sudi's sister, formerly known as Oceana. "But to look at him, you'd think he's a bum."

Nico can smell the pee, hopes the dog doesn't have any other business to do.

Anthony runs a hand through his long and very black hair. "Do you know anything about odour?"

Nico's head snaps up.

Sudi looks at Nico. "Well," she says, "a little, I guess."

"I have a condition called hyperosmia," says Anthony. "Basically, it's a heightened sense of smell."

"Every year," says Cleopatra, "the companies that make deodorants and mouthwash and foot powder and genital sprays hire people like Anthony to test the effectiveness of their products."

"That's me," says Anthony.

Nico says nothing. Keeps his eyes on the dog.

"So, you . . ."

And this is as far as Sudi gets.

"Right," says Anthony. "I smell people's breath and their armpits and their feet to see if the products are effective."

Nico has to admire the man. He says all this with a straight face.

"Most people think it's a joke," says Anthony. "But odour is a billion-dollar industry."

"And now that aliens have landed on the moon," says Cleopatra, "Anthony is going to be raking it in."

"Alien odours are going to be the new growth sector," says Anthony.

Sudi nods. "So, you two are getting married."

"We are," says Anthony.

"Congratulations."

"That's what we want to talk to you about," says Cleopatra.

"We're getting married in New Zealand," says Anthony. "Wharariki Beach, South Island."

"It's west of Abel Tasman National Park," says Cleopatra.

"Wedding on a beach," says Sudi. "Sounds nice."

"After the last year," says Cleopatra, "something nice will be welcome."

Nico hopes that Sudi is not going to ask her sister for the details. And she doesn't. Not that this stops Cleopatra. For the next twenty minutes, the Queen of the Nile treats Nico and Sudi to a clown-car fire drill of a life that features several men, a divorce, a vandalized trailer, a startup company, and a problem with banks.

"That's what we want to talk to you about."

Nico doesn't ask. Neither does Sudi.

"CLAN," says Cleopatra. "It's the first two letters of our names."

Sudi nods.

"It's a virtual company," says Anthony. "So, there's no physical plant or any of the costs associated with a brick-and-mortar business."

Nico nods.

"But we have to generate investment interest before the bank will provide the initial startup monies."

"For the computers and the servers and the salaries of the technical personnel," says Anthony.

"We want you to be there at the beginning," says Cleopatra.

Sudi keeps her voice flat and blunted. "You want us to lend you money?"

"Not a loan," says Cleopatra. "An investment in the future."

"And, of course," says Anthony, "we want you to come to the wedding."

THAT EVENING, SUDI WARMS up leftover chicken for dinner. Nico opens a bottle of wine. A red that received a rating of ninety-eight and wasn't all that expensive.

"So, what do you think?"

Nico had hoped to avoid this conversation.

"New Zealand might be an interesting place for a vacation," says Sudi.

"And while we're there," says Nico, "we can go to their wedding?"

"Two birds," says Sudi. "And then there's the investment in the future."

Nico isn't sure what the future is or why everyone expects it to be better than the present. Or the past, for that matter. So far as he can tell, the future is little more than an expression of optimism, a fantasy to avoid the despair of today.

"Seven and a half billion people in the world right now? By 2050, the estimate is for ten billion."

Nico twists spaghetti onto his fork, waits for the number to sink in.

"We think society is in trouble now? Think jobs are hard to find now? Think the housing market is inflated now? Think climate change will go away anytime soon? Think wars are a thing of the past?"

"Have some more wine."

"Maybe that's why the aliens are on the moon."

Sudi smiles a sad smile.

"Or maybe it's their version of a destination vacation," says Nico. "They've come for the Global Destruction Derby. Sit on the moon and watch as humanity annihilates itself. Along with the planet. Limited seating. Enjoy the spectacle from a safe distance."

Nico can feel his mind and body warming to the task when he's interrupted by a car pulling into the driveway. Most of the time, it's people turning around.

"It's the aliens," he tells Sudi. "Come to save us from ourselves."

Sudi stops eating. "I think it's a police car."

It is a police car. And it's parked in the driveway. Nico runs through the possibilities that could have brought the law to his door.

The bees.

That's it. There's a bylaw that protects bees from assault, and someone reported him. Why can't the little insects chew on the fence? He could live with that.

The officer who gets out of the car is a young woman. From a distance, she looks to be twelve.

"Good evening. Nico Karras?" Now that she is up close, Nico can see that she's not twelve. "I'm Constable Inez Sanchez."

She's at least fourteen.

Constable Sanchez is wearing a thick bullet-proof vest, a heavy utility belt that bristles with a gun, a flashlight, and what looks to be an aerosol can that is not deodorant. Nico imagines that all the gear is necessary in Sanchez's line of work, but the outfit makes her look as though she's stepped into a fat suit for a cameo in a police comedy.

"It's the bees. Right?"

"Bees?"

"You wouldn't believe the damage they do."

"Would it be possible to talk inside?"

Sudi is waiting at the table.

"This is Inspector Sanchez."

"Constable," says Sanchez. "Have you had a conversation with . . ." Sanchez takes out her cellphone. ". . . a Ms. Darby Dock?"

Nico looks at Sudi. Sudi looks at Nico.

"She is the director at Autumn Leaves."

"Wait. Is this about my mother?"

Sanchez consults her phone. "Mrs. Thea Karras."

"That's my mother," says Nico. "What's happened?"

"So, you haven't talked to Ms. Dock?"

Nico tries to remember what Darby Dock looks like and comes up empty. He must have met her when he and his mother toured the facility, must have sat across from her when he filled out the paperwork, wrote the initial cheque.

"No," says Nico. "Haven't talked to her."

"So, you don't know that your mother is missing?"

Sudi sits up straight. "His mother is missing?"

"Evidently, there was a trip to the mall," says Sanchez. "Mrs. Karras was on the bus when it went to the mall, but she wasn't on the bus when it returned."

Sanchez pauses, swipes a finger across the screen. "Actually, the bus broke down and everyone was taken back to the retirement centre in taxis, and somehow your mother got lost in the shuffle."

Nico knows he's not going to hear the end of this, can already hear his mother's voice.

This wouldn't have happened if I was living in my own home.

This wouldn't happen if I had a daughter.

This wouldn't have happened if you had given me grandchildren.

Nico looks at his watch. "How long has she been missing?"

"Since Saturday," says Sanchez. "Ms. Dock only filed a missing-person report this morning. We were hoping that your mother might have come here."

"No," says Sudi. "We didn't know she was missing."

"Three days?" says Nico. "Three days?"

"Here's my number." Sanchez hands Nico a card. "Call me any time for an update."

"She's an old woman," says Nico. "She forgets things."

"My *abuela* is the same." Sanchez nods sympathetically. "But we still love them."

Nico waits until Constable Sanchez leaves.

"Three days!"

"Getting all worked up isn't going to help."

"I'm not worked up," says Nico. "I'm mad as hell."

"And that won't help either."

"Fucking Autumn Leaves loses my mother, and they don't bother to tell me?"

"Certainly seems an oversight."

"Oversight? It's criminal." Nico walks to the refrigerator, and then he walks back. "Good mind to sue them."

"Now you sound like an American," says Sudi. "It's not pretty."

"Three days. She's probably dead somewhere."

Sudi guides Nico to the sofa, sits him down, sits down next to him. "Your mother's not dead. She's tough. She's probably at a restaurant somewhere having coffee, wondering what all the fuss is about."

"I don't know what to do."

"Well," says Sudi, "why don't you get your hat. We'll drive to the mall, see if she's still there. There are places to eat and bathrooms as well. Not to mention the vibrating chairs across from Sport Chek. You can sit in those chairs for hours. And that bookstore. A person can get lost in that bookstore."

NICO HASN'T BEEN TO the mall in ages. They're not one of his favourite places. One mall is like another mall, and after you've seen two or three, they all run together.

"You know what malls don't have?"

"I hope this isn't a negative comment," says Sudi. "We need to stay positive."

"Hardware stores," says Nico. "And golf stores. Car dealerships."

"There was a car dealership at the West Edmonton Mall. And a big amusement park."

"One exception doesn't disprove the rule." Nico finds the vibrating chairs and sits down. "No big department stores anymore."

"Mark's Work Wearhouse," says Sudi.

"No grocery stores."

"But it does have theatres, arcades, food courts."

"Place feels like a giant dollar store."

Nico leans back in the chair. He thinks about putting a loonie in the coin slot. But the chair doesn't take a loonie. The damn thing wants a toonie. Nico can't believe it. Who's going to pay two dollars for a little shaking?

Sudi sits in the chair next to him. "You know, your mother doesn't like me."

"She doesn't like anyone."

"It's because we don't have children," says Sudi. "And she blames me."

"We don't have children because neither of us wanted children."

"She doesn't understand that."

"Then let's not find her." Nico pushes out of the chair. "Let's go home."

Sudi stays where she is. "We have to find her," she tells Nico. "The one thing has little to do with the other."

THAT NIGHT, NICO CAN'T sleep. He gets up to pee, discovers that he's wide awake. And angry. Angry with his mother. Angry with his car. Angry with the bees that are destroying his house.

He finds a fly swatter, goes out into the backyard. The moon is full in the sky. The night air has cooled. Nico stands in the dark in his pyjama bottoms and T-shirt and beats, beats, beats the swatter against the cedar fascia.

Until the head snaps off.

Herb has discovered one of the downsides to owning a drive-in. People can see the movie playing on the screen from the road and think the place is open. The neon rocket all lit up against the sky doesn't help either. Even the Launch Pad has a welcoming glow leaking out the windows.

Mind you, Herb has finally chained and locked the front gate, has nailed a sign to the ticket booth.

Closed Forever.

In large capitals.

That should be a clue to any passing cinephile. And yet people still pull in, park next to the ticket booth, stand on top of their cars for a better view of the screen and the lot. A few of the more adventurous have scaled the fence, wandered the grounds, taking selfies and the like.

One guy had a camera on a stick. He was doing a podcast, he told Herb. On drive-ins. How they were a forgotten piece of a lost social civilization and a precursor in the evolution of the cellphone as theatre and the individual as god.

Herb has tried to be generous.

Herb has set up a makeshift patio about fifty yards back from the screen. Table, chair, umbrella. Next to the Astroturf tee box he has made out of plywood and carpet and a stand he has banged together for his clubs. Couple of books on the table, if he feels like reading, and a cooler with soft drinks and healthy low-fat snacks.

Tonight, he doesn't feel like doing anything. He's watched all the movies that came with the place at least half a dozen times, has considered buying some new ones. And because he hasn't picked up the balls from his last practice session, he has nothing to hit.

Been here long enough.

There was a round-table discussion on PBS the night before about longevity and how human life expectancy is influenced, in part, by epigenetic mechanisms. The talking heads spent a good deal of time on the science of the matter and almost no time on the elemental question.

Was extended longevity a good idea?

Given the tumble and throw of human history, Herb can see an excellent argument being made for reducing the lifespans of *Homo sapiens*. Living longer has not made humans any smarter, has not made them any more compassionate, has not made them more generous, has not made them less full of themselves and their imagined place in the world.

More people living longer, it follows, would simply make the situation worse.

As it has.

Besides, what would one do with an extra twenty or thirty years that they hadn't already done in the preceding seventy? What would Herb do? Hit more balls at more movies?

There's a news report on an alien spacecraft that has purportedly landed on the Blood reserve in Alberta. With video of a camera crew trying to get onto the reserve and being turned away by a blockade. Herb watches the video closely to see if he can spot any friends or relatives, and sure enough, there's his cousin, Leroy Day Chief, looking older, standing at the front of the barricade.

How long has it been? Twenty? Thirty years? Before he met Katherine. They had gone back once. For his mother's funeral. Katherine had asked him if he would be happier living in Alberta, closer to the reserve and his family, and Herb had told her that he was fine living in Ontario.

Now, having seen Leroy on television, Herb thinks he might call, say hello, hear his cousin's voice and easy laugh.

The night settles in, soft and velvet. A cloudless sky. The stars overhead. The land curled up around him.

Herb has no idea if the old number he has for Leroy is still good.

The phone rings, and then it rings some more, and more after that. If it goes to an answering machine, Herb will just hang up and get on with life.

"*Oki.*"

Leroy's voice. No mistaking it for anyone else.

"Leroy . . ."

"Hey, that you, cousin?"

Herb takes a deep breath.

"Where are you? You in town?"

"No, I'm still here in Ontario." Herb looks up at the big screen. "Saw you on television."

Leroy's laugh comes tumbling down the line, a warm flow that washes over him.

"You looked good."

"Was supposed to look fierce," says Leroy. "But I just looked old."

"So, you guys got an alien spacecraft?"

Another laugh.

"Don't tell anyone," says Leroy.

"It was on the news," says Herb. "Think they already know."

"You remember Danny Many Horses?"

"Martin's brother?"

"Yep. Danny was hauling a hopper bin over to Cardston, buried a tire on the shoulder, tipped the load over. Some guy took a photo of the bin lying on its side, sent it to the *Herald*."

"You're kidding."

"Nope," says Leroy. "Any idiot can see that it's a hopper bin for a grain silo, but who's going to listen to reason when aliens are more fun."

"So, no alien spacecraft?"

"Hell yes, it's a spaceship." Herb can hear the wink in Leroy's voice. "Got a bunch of suits flying in tomorrow. They want access to the craft. We want to talk about the land claim."

Herb smiles, leans back, looks for Ihkitsikammiksi in the night sky.

"How's the family?"

"Good," says Leroy. "You should come home. Hang out with the Niitsitapi."

"The real people."

"See. You haven't forgotten."

"Maybe I will."

"Maybe's not an answer," says Leroy. "Sun Dance is in a couple of weeks. Come on out. We'll have our lodge up. You can stay with us."

Herb snorts. "You just want me to buy groceries and carry wood."

"Come for the Indians, stay for the aliens." Leroy is laughing again. "Cultural tourism. The new buffalo of vacations. Number one on Tripadvisor."

BY THE TIME HERB and Leroy wrap up the call, the battery indicator on Herb's phone shows the charge at ten percent. He'll have to remember to plug it in tonight.

Strange how talking to someone from his past can make Herb feel alive. Maybe he will go to the Sun Dance. Fly to Calgary, drive the two and a half hours to the reserve. Stay with Leroy's family. Go from lodge to lodge, drinking tea, telling stories, hanging out. What did he have to keep him here? A defunct drive-in-cum-driving-range? A snack shack of a house? A neon rocket that doesn't go anywhere?

Memories?

If he does go, he could put cartoons on a continuous loop. If the aliens can see the screen from the moon, they'll get a kick out of watching Coyote chase the Roadrunner, Elmer Fudd chase Bugs Bunny, Tom chase Jerry.

Herb gets out of the chair, grabs a seven-iron from the bag, lines the club up for a high fade.

"Turn around and you're a dead man."

Herb turns around.

"I told you not to turn around."

A man. More a kid. Jeans and a T-shirt, with what looks to be a flag of some sort wrapped around his face and head. And a gun. A small black gun.

"And drop the fucking golf club."

"Billy?"

"What? No."

"Billy Kiddle," says Herb. "You work for Chuck, right?"

"No, I don't," says Billy. "Give me all your cash."

"Is that a starter's pistol?" Herb gently swings the club from side to side. "Are you trying to rob me?"

"And your health card." Billy waves the pistol at Herb. "And your passport."

Herb makes a slow, full swing with the seven-iron. "You brought a starter's pistol to a driving range?"

"Driving range?" Billy looks around. "This is a fucking drive-in."

"You ever been hit with a golf club?" Herb holds the club out in front of him so Billy can see the heavy metal head. "If the shaft were steel, it might bend, but this one is graphite."

Billy keeps the pistol pointed at Herb. But he takes a step back. "You want to die, old man?"

Greek. Herb is pretty sure that the flag that Billy has wrapped around his head and face is Greek.

"There's soft drinks in the cooler." Herb puts the club back in the bag, sits down in the chair. "And some chocolate chip cookies."

Which reminds Billy that he hasn't eaten.

"What kind of soft drinks?"

"Look for yourself."

Billy lifts the lid of the cooler. "Make any funny moves, and you're dead."

Herb folds his hands on his chest, closes his eyes. "You ever robbed anyone before?"

"Killed the last guy 'cause he wouldn't listen." Billy finds a Pepsi. "So, what about that cash? I'll bet you have a lot of cash stashed away."

"Thousands," says Herb. "But I'm so old, I've forgotten where I put it."

"Hey," says Billy. "You think I'm fooling around?"

"I do," says Herb. "Have a cookie."

Billy discovers that he can't drink the Pepsi or eat the cookie with the flag wrapped around his head.

"You knew it was me 'cause I helped you clean this place out when you first moved in."

"That's right."

"Shit." Billy takes a second cookie. "Guessing you're not going to give me your money."

"I'm not."

"Or your health card."

"Certainly not," says Herb. "Nor am I giving you my passport."

"Okay." Billy puts the gun in his pocket. "It's a starter's pistol. But it looks real."

"Not really," says Herb. "Why are you trying to rob me?"

"Duh," says Billy. "Money. I'm broke. Chuck don't need me 'cause the aliens have fucked up real estate."

"You ever play golf?"

Billy shakes his head. "Rich man's thing."

"True enough," says Herb. "You want to give it a try?"

HERB HAS BILLY HELP him pick up balls. Then he shows him how to hold the club, how to make the swing.

"Forget about the ball," Herb tells him. "Just make the swing as though the ball isn't there."

The first couple of times, Billy misses the ball completely.

"Don't swing so hard. Smooth and slow. Let the club do all the work."

Billy tops the next dozen.

"Better," says Herb. "Even slower."

By the end of an hour, Billy is hitting the balls solid. They fly off the tee and into the night.

"Damn." Herb shakes his head. "You're a natural."

Billy is shaking with excitement. "How far you think I hit that one?"

"Doesn't matter how far you hit it," says Herb. "More important to hit it where you want to hit it."

"This is what you do all day?" Billy shakes his head. "You must be some kind of depressed."

Herb and Billy take a break, walk out to the screen, gather up more balls.

"You think I could be a golfer?"

"Probably can't be a crook and a golfer at the same time."

"Not really a crook," says Billy. "I never killed anyone."

"I figured," says Herb.

"I *have* robbed a bunch of people."

"Probably have to stop doing that if you want to be a golfer."

Billy carries the bucket of balls back to the makeshift patio. Sets it down next to the Astroturf tee box.

"My girlfriend thinks I'm a loser."

Herb looks up at the screen. "You like westerns?"

Billy nods. "Sure. Who doesn't like westerns."

Herb takes a moment to think it through. "I'm going to go away for a while. Don't know how long I'll be gone."

"You sick or something?"

Herb shakes his head. "No. I have to go to Alberta. And while I'm gone, I could use someone to look after the drive-in."

"You offering me a job?"

"I am."

"A paying job?"

"I'd need you to live here. You think you could do that?"

"I could live here rent-free? Watch movies and hit golf balls?"

"You could."

"Could I bring Darlene out?" Billy turns around in a circle. "She's my girlfriend."

"The one who's upset with you?"

Billy can't believe his luck. Looking after the drive-in would be perfect. He doesn't think that Darlene ratted him out to the cops, but if she did, the Lunar is the perfect place for a hideout.

"I was supposed to pick her up at the hospital," says Billy. "I'm in deep shit."

Herb holds out a hand. "So," he says, "do we have a deal?"

XVI

Richard Dock, Dick to his family, is in the small park over-looking Fisherman's Wharf, talking with Ed and Freddy the dog. The sky is high and blue, puffy breeze off the water, a brilliant west-coast day.

Ed is again urging Dick to do a feature story on cruise ships. "About time someone ripped the scab off that wound."

Dick isn't sure what wound Ed is talking about, but he likes the man's enthusiasm and his unwavering conviction. Maybe he should forget about e-bikes and return to an exposé on the big ships.

"Put a couple of the aliens onboard the *Irony of the Seas*," says Ed. "Shake the bag. See what happens."

From the park, Dick can see Carla Tupper on the upper deck of her houseboat. She has her For Sale sign up again and is stretched out on the lounge chair in her sundress and hat.

From a distance, she looks like the rich girlfriend that Dick wishes he had. So far, his online dating has been a bust. There don't appear to be many rich women looking for intelligent and compassionate boyfriends. Just a bunch of poor women looking for rich boyfriends.

And what choices there are have not been encouraging.

"So, maybe instead of an exposé," says Ed, "you could write a short story. Aliens on a cruise ship. Aliens eating the passengers. They make movies out of less."

Freddy the dog has just done his business on the grass, a visual reminder that Dick does not want a pet. Ed picks up the poop in a little green bag, twirls it around, ties it in a knot.

"Hey," he says, "look at that."

Dick turns to see what Ed sees, but he doesn't see it at first. And then he does. A man in front of the Lagoon, hammering a For Sale sign into the grass.

"People are trying to sell their places before the aliens invade," says Ed. "There are six more signs up at Shoal Point."

Maybe Dick should do a story on the cost of condos and the impact of an alien invasion on the real estate business.

"I'm off for two weeks," says Ed. "Sheila and I are going to go to Winnipeg. She wants to move there."

"Winnipeg?"

"Yeah," says Ed. "It's not my idea of a good time."

"You'd leave Victoria?"

"It's pretty expensive here," says Ed. "And it's not going to get any cheaper."

Dick can't imagine living anywhere else.

"Freddy isn't going to like the snow and the cold. But he's a dog and doesn't get a vote."

Dick watches the real estate agent with the sign. He's doing a fine job of pounding the stake into the ground.

"Talk more when we get back." Ed gives Freddy's leash a shake. "Look forward to reading the article."

The real estate man has just finished pounding and adjusting. The sign stands up nice and straight. It's a fine sign if Dick does say so, all clean and sparkling in the sunlight.

"Hello." Dick takes a card out of his pocket, holds it out. "Richard Dock. *Camosack: Victoria's Lifestyle Magazine.*"

The man looks at the card. Hands Dick one of his own.

"Jim Regan," says the man. "Re/Max."

"Condo for sale, eh?"

"A real beauty. One bedroom. View of the harbour. It will be gone in a week."

"I live in the building," says Dick. "One bedroom, view of the harbour. What's the asking price?"

Regan tells him. Dick blows a low whistle, makes a note to self to let Darby know how much the condo has appreciated under his watchful eye.

"You know anyone interested in a great unit," says Regan, "give them my name."

DICK CHECKS THE MAILBOX in the lobby. Four letters. One is from the City of Victoria. The second is from the homeowners' association. The third letter is addressed to "Resident." It's an application for a credit card. Dick gets these each month.

The fourth letter is from his sister.

He'll open the letters later. Right now, he has to decide on lunch. He'd like to eat out more often. That's what famous people do. And eating out is one of the most effective ways to meet famous people. Nelly Furtado at Aura. Hugh Jackman at Fathom. Stephen King at Q in the Empress.

Stop by the table with a business card. Richard Dock. Editor-in-chief of *Camosack: Victoria's Lifestyle Magazine.* Dick is sure that famous people will want to meet him. He's confident that they will want to be interviewed and photographed.

But if he's going to meet famous people, he's going to have to be able to eat out. He's explained all this to his sister, but so far, Darby has refused to increase his allowance.

So, today it will have to be leftover chicken and rice. At home.

Dick sits at the table and watches the seaplane land in the harbour. In a little while, it will take off again, fly away to Vancouver and to the smaller communities on the island. Comox and Campbell River. Tofino and Port Hardy. Watching the seaplane always brings out a longing in him. He'd like to travel. See the world. Go to all the exotic places.

Not that the exotic places want people coming anymore. Venice, Lanzarote, Bali, Santorini are actively discouraging visitors. Activists in Amsterdam are pushing tourists into canals. Angry locals in Barcelona are spraying tourists with water pistols.

And Victoria? Now that Dick thinks about it, he hasn't heard any talk about curtailing tourism in Victoria. No rumours of matrons from Oak Bay with YANKEE GO HOME placards, chasing Americans down the street.

No, Dick decides, Victoria is a peaceable kingdom. Where you can stroll through a vast flower garden, putt around the harbour in a water taxi, watch whales from the safety of a rubber boat.

Victoria. Where lions can lie down with lambs.

The letter from the City of Victoria is a notice that there has been an increase in property taxes. Dick shakes his head. Darby is not going to like that. She's already expressed her disapproval of the current taxes on the condo.

The second letter from the homeowners' association is a bill for the increase in property taxes and a one-time assessment to cover the cost of repairs to the physical plant. Whatever that means. Dick doesn't know exactly what needs to be repaired, but it's certainly expensive. He can hear his sister's reaction to this.

The third letter offers a free credit card, which Dick knows is an oxymoron. Credit cards aren't free. Only a fool would think that they were free. And Dick is no fool.

The last letter is from Darby. His birthday is less than a month away, so there's a chance that it's a present. A gift card. For a cellphone. Except it's not. It's simply a letter. No happy birthday. No gift card. No money.

Just a letter.

Dear Dick, I'm selling the condo. Love, Darby.

Dick reads the letter again. And then a third time.

And then he smiles. Of course. It's a scam. He's read about things such as this. Darby would never sell the condo. It's his home. It's where he lives, where he works. If she sells the condo, he wouldn't have anywhere to live, and that's not fair. He'd be on the street. Like Tanis Hoplin. Riding around on a red scooter, hustling the tourists.

Is that the kind of life Darby wants for her brother? Homeless? A cellphone is one thing.

The real estate man with the sign. Was the For Sale sign for his condo? Dick reads the letter a fourth time.

Dear Dick, I'm selling the condo. Love, Darby.

Dick, not Richard. Only the family calls him Dick. So, the letter is real. My god, my god, my god. Dick says this out loud. My home. You can't sell my home. Can't, can't, can't.

Dick will have to call Darby immediately. Explain to her why selling the condo is impossible. He'll have to write the reasons down so he can give them to her in the proper order.

Number one. She can't sell something that isn't hers. Yes, it's legally hers, but there is a moral component at work here, and morally, the condo belongs to him. He'll need to work on number one, but he'll do that later, when he's had time to edit the complete list.

He's working on number two when there's a knock at the door. Dick isn't expecting anyone, doesn't want to see anyone at this moment, is much too busy to entertain another person.

Through the fish eye in the door, Dick can see a woman standing in the hallway. The woman from the other evening. At the homeowners' meeting. Betty or Barbara or Brenda.

"Oh, good, you're home."

"I am."

"Miranda," says the woman. "Miranda Lansky."

"Richard," says Dick. "Richard Dock."

Miranda smiles. "I know who you are."

"And you can see me?"

"Your condo," says Miranda, "I understand it's for sale."

Dick can see that he needs to stop the rumour before it gets out of hand.

"No, it's not."

"No?"

Dick sets his feet firmly on the threshold, digs his toes into the carpet. "No."

"Oh," says Miranda, as though she's just been given bad news. "It's just that Lillian . . . Lillian Bancroft, a friend, a very good friend, in fact. Lilly lives in Prince George and her husband died, and Prince George is not the safest place to live, and Lilly wants to come to Victoria."

Dick braces the door frame with his arms. He's seen the statistics for crime in Prince George. Lilly is right to be worried.

"She wants someplace peaceful and quiet, and when I heard about the sale, I called Lilly, and she's coming down to see the place. She's already talked to the agent."

"My place?"

"I think it's your sister's place." Miranda looks sympathetic. "Anyway, we were hoping that we could get rid of the agent and buy the property direct. That way, Lilly would save money and your sister would save money."

Dick can feel the anger rising up through his body. This is the kind of anger, he supposes, that turns pleasant people into serial killers.

"Do you think that would be possible?"

Dick explains, once more, that the condo is not for sale, that his sister has made a mistake, and that the matter will all be straightened out in the morning.

"Would nine o'clock be convenient?" asks Miranda. "Just a quick peek. I think she's really going to like it."

Dick shuts and locks the door, goes immediately to the phone and dials his sister's number.

"You've reached Darby Dock. Leave a message and I'll get back to you."

Dick hangs up and dials again.

"You've reached Darby Dock. Leave a message and I'll get back to you."

And again.

And again.

And again.

The walk around the quay and along Government Street is fraught with dark thoughts, and he finds himself unable to concentrate on the magazine or rich girlfriends.

Or cellphones, for that matter.

All he can think about is his condo, and how his sister intends to sell it out from under him. Where will he go? A doorway? A steam grate on Fort? What will he do? Ride around in circles on a red scooter? What is Darby thinking?

The Orca is quiet. Dick orders a macchiato, takes it to a table at the back. Where he can hide in the shadows. Where he can practise being invisible.

"Hey."

Dick looks up. It's Bradley.

"Stanley," says the man. "Stanley Bulger. Rich asshole? No fiancée?"

Of course Dick remembers him.

Stanley sits down. The man has shaved. He's showered. His eyes are no longer red. They're bright and alive.

"I am so glad we ran into each other again." Stanley pauses, like a diver on a high board. "Guess what?"

Dick smiles.

"Amity," says Stanley. "My fiancée? She wants me back. You believe it?"

Dick sips his macchiato.

"Out of the blue, I get a phone call. She's crying. Says she overreacted. Hormones. Aliens. Doesn't matter. Is that great or is that great?"

Dick agrees that it's great.

"Such good fortune," says Stanley. "I meet you, and Amity changes her mind."

Dick could use some good fortune of his own right about now.

"Amity wants to go to Thailand. Wants to sail around the Similan Islands."

Dick has heard that Thailand is nice.

"So, that's what we're going to do."

Dick nods his approval, takes another sip of his espresso.

"I'm flying to Dallas tonight. She's going to meet me at the airport." Stanley reaches out, lays a hand on Dick's shoulder in benediction. "I don't know how to thank you."

THE FOLLOWING EVENING, DICK is on the upper deck of the *Splendour of the Seas*, enjoying a glass of wine and watching the lights of the houses along Dallas Road twinkle in the dusk.

As it turns out, Stanley *did* find a way to thank him.

"I can't use it," Stanley told him in the Orca. "And what's the point in letting it go to waste?"

Dick agreed that waste was bad.

"I've only been on board since San Francisco, and all of that time, I stayed in my stateroom. I was pretty depressed."

Dick knows that depression is a serious condition.

"So, no one really knows me. We look enough like each other, and you'll have my lanyard and ID card. No harm, no foul."

Dick does see the resemblance.

"I can't give you my passport, but once you're on board, you won't need one."

Dick tries to remember if he even has a passport.

"And I'll even throw in some money, so you can take a couple of the excursions, buy a souvenir or two. You'll have a great time. And maybe you'll meet your very own Amity on the cruise."

And in the end, Dick could see no reason to say no.

SO HERE HE IS, Richard Dock, Dick to his family, aboard a cruise ship bound for exotic places. He sits on deck, feels the ship move under him as it leaves port and slowly heads for the open ocean.

Lobster is on the menu for dinner and there's a floor show, a Las Vegas review with an ABBA cover band and a magician. Followed by a late-night aliens-on-the-moon viewing from the bow of the ship.

Binoculars supplied by the cruise line.

Tomorrow and the next day are cruising days with nothing to do but sit in a deck chair and watch the world float by.

And now that he has had time to think about it, Dick realizes that Darby isn't selling the condo in order to put him on the street. She's selling the unit so she can upgrade to a single-family house on South Turner. She's seen the wisdom of his real-estate advice. If the internet connection on the ship is good enough, he'll look up the listings, send suggestions to his sister, so she doesn't make a poor choice.

A bungalow rather than a two-storey. As he gets older, stairs are sure to be a problem.

The wind has freshened and cooled. Dick sits on the balcony of his stateroom, a deck blanket wrapped around his shoulders, and watches the moon float in the night sky. He'll try to remember to send Darby a postcard when they get to wherever they're going.

He wouldn't want her to worry.

In the meantime, he'll finish up the premiere issue of *Camosack* with its double-page feature. "World Cruises in the Time of Interstellar Uncertainty." Along with a shorter article on the hazards of e-bikes.

But first, what he really needs is a cellphone.

XVII

Chuck Mason has not had a good run lately. His real estate business is in free fall.

On the rental side, he owns seven properties. Only three of which are rented. Two are being repaired, and the other two are occupied by deadbeats who won't pay the rent. He'd like to forcibly evict them, but they've filed a suit with the Landlord and Tenant Board, and that bureaucratic circus will waste at least five months of his time.

Okay, there are some minor plumbing and air-conditioning problems, and he did change the locks on the two-storey on Douglas.

On the real estate side, he has twenty-six houses on listing, and if a couple of them sell, he'll get some help with his cash-flow problem. But right now, none of the properties is being shown, and there are no offers.

Everyone is standing pat, waiting to see what the aliens on the moon are going to do. What the hell does it matter what they do? Prices are low. Interest rates are low. Now's the time to make a move.

You can't live in a cave the rest of your life.

And now, on top of all that, Billy Kiddle has disappeared. With Chuck's pickup. The perfect end to the perfect week.

The only bright spot on a black horizon is a developer out of Toronto who is looking for acreage in the area suitable for a condo/retail complex.

And Chuck knows just the spot.

Then there's his ex-wife. Darby Mason, though she's no longer Darby Mason. When the divorce was finalized, Darby went back to her maiden name.

Dock.

Stupid name. Darby Dock. Tick tock. Donald Duck.

Chuck doesn't understand women who do that. It's as though they think they can turn back time or erase history. You get married, you change your name, that's it. Marriage is like branding cattle, Chuck has joked with her. And he has the branding iron.

There's another potential source of income. The condo in Victoria. It's true that Darby had it before they were married, so it wasn't included in the divorce settlement, but now that she is going to sell it, there's no reason why he shouldn't share in the profits. They were married for almost twelve years. Some of his money went into maintaining the condo and Darby's deadbeat brother. He's entitled to some level of return.

He's certainly not going to get rich playing five bucks a hole with the golfing cabal. So, in the meantime, unless he can pull a daisy out of his ass, he's fucked.

Herb Good Runner. Potential daisy.

When the developer from Toronto came calling, Chuck knew beyond certainty that the Lunar Drive-in would fit the bill perfectly. Twenty-two acres of flat land on the edge of town. Take down the screen, doze the snack shack, level the land.

Yes, the zoning hasn't been changed, but with a project of the magnitude that the developer was describing, the city council isn't going to say no. A little cash spread around here and there. A done deal if there ever was one.

All Chuck has to do is convince Herb to sell. Which shouldn't be a huge problem. Surely the man is tired of hitting golf balls up against the movie screen. Surely he's tired of living alone in a drive-in snack shack.

But with contraries, you never know.

Chuck figures it's all in the way he presents the idea. Maybe start with what Herb would like to do with the rest of his life.

Travel?

Everyone likes to travel. With the money from the sale, Herb could travel around the world first class.

Or what about a nice house in a nice neighbourhood? A cottage on a lake? A cute little *pied-à-terre* in the city. Chuck can help with any of the above. In fact, he has several properties for sale right this minute that would fit the bill.

And if travel or real estate doesn't float Herb's boat, there are lots of other ways to have a good time. Fancy cars. Luxury cruises. Women. Women are a surefire way to enjoy a pile of cash.

But what if Herb doesn't want to sell? He's always been a bit of a strange duck. Even when Katherine was alive. What if he's content living in a drive-in? Only one way to find out. Chuck could call, but he's found that real estate is always better discussed face to face.

As Chuck drives to the Lunar, he considers his approaches. Best not to ask Herb if he wants to sell the place. Best to suggest that selling is a done deal. Tell Herb that he has an offer in hand, all cash, some ridiculous figure, just a few details to iron out.

All you have to do is sign the representation agreement.

Right here.

On that line.

Doesn't matter that Chuck doesn't have an actual offer in hand. Once he's the broker of record, he can go to the developer with the plot map. Here's exactly what you're looking for. Lots of interest. Won't last long. Yes, we'd entertain a bully offer.

By the time Chuck gets to the ticket booth, he's made the sale and is spending the commission. The last time he was here, the gate was open. Now it's locked and chained. The big screen is dark, but Chuck can see lights on in the Launch Pad. So, Herb is home.

Chuck debates shouting or blowing his horn, but he's not sure that that will set the proper tone, not sure sudden noises will put Herb in the mood to listen to a terrific offer. Best to come in gentle, best to come in friendly.

The fence is not that high. A younger man could use his strength and agility to scale it easily. Chuck uses his brain, pulls up alongside, climbs onto the roof of his car, rolls over the top of the fence, and drops into the drive-in.

A fifty-year-old ninja on finasteride and statins.

One torn pant leg. Slivers in his hands. A tweaked ankle. He won't do that again.

The walk from the fence to the Launch Pad is over uneven ground, and Chuck can feel each step, as he limps up and down the swales. He'll add a bonus for himself to the commission. Damage to pants. Injury to body. An extra two percent. Maybe three.

Better solution than a lawsuit. Nobody wants that.

The door to the Launch Pad is wide open. The lights are on, the popcorn machine is up and running, the TV is playing in the background.

"Hello."

Chuck stands in the doorway, strikes a pose that suggests honesty and good cheer.

"Hello."

Somewhere in the back of the snack shack, a toilet flushes, and in that instant, Chuck realizes that if Herb comes out of the bathroom and sees him standing there, it might startle the man.

Which will not do.

Chuck quickly backs out of the doorway, walks out into the lot and the night, and waits. Through the window, he can see a figure moving about.

"Hello." Chuck turns his head away from the shack, so it seems as though he's off at a distance. "It's me. Chuck. Chuck Mason."

Chuck can't make out the figure that comes to the doorway, stands with the light at his back.

"Chuck?"

Chuck knows that whiny voice. It's not Herb.

"Billy?"

"Chuck?"

Chuck makes his way to the shack. What the hell is going on?

"Why are you limping?"

Chuck pushes past Billy, heads straight to the sofa, flops down, throws his leg up onto the coffee table.

"Where's Herb?"

"How'd you get in?"

Billy Kiddle? Billy is the last person Chuck expects to find at the drive-in.

"What'd you do with Herb?"

"What? Nothing."

"Why are you here?"

"I'm working," says Billy. "Got a full-time job."

"Job?"

"Watching the place," says Billy. "Herb left me in charge."

Chuck has trouble imagining Billy in charge of anything. "Where'd he go?"

"Not sure I can tell you."

"And where's my pickup?"

"Okay, okay," says Billy. "Hold your horses. Think he went to Alberta."

"Think?"

"Yeah, he went to Alberta."

"He say why?"

Billy wanders over to the popcorn machine. "Nope."

"He say when he's coming back?"

"Double nope."

"Shit."

"You want some popcorn?"

Chuck closes his eyes, tries not to think about his ankle, tries to figure out what to do next.

"You got any way to reach him?"

"You mean like a cellphone?"

The music on the TV takes a kick in volume. On the screen, a metal giant is standing in front of a spaceship.

"Did you hear?" Billy points to the set. "The aliens have invaded. Started about half an hour ago."

"Aliens?"

"The ones who were on the moon." Billy comes around the counter with a bag of popcorn. "See that giant robot? It's going to destroy the earth if we don't do what the aliens say."

Chuck watches the TV. Patricia Neal is talking to Michael Rennie.

"That's not an invasion," says Chuck. "That's a movie."

"That's what they want you to think."

"That's *The Day the Earth Stood Still.*" Chuck tries to remember when it was made. Was it 1950, 1951?

Billy eats a mouthful of popcorn. "Right."

"There was a remake around 2007. It wasn't nearly as good as the original."

"It's pretty smart," says Billy. "Film the invasion and pretend it's a movie. By the time we realize what's happening, it's too late."

Chuck rubs his forehead. What the hell is he going to do? He can't sell the drive-in without Herb, and Herb is gone with no return date. The developer isn't going to wait forever. If Chuck can't give him something, he'll find someone else.

"So, Herb left you in charge?"

Billy nods.

"Okay, here's what I need you to do. Tomorrow, I'm going to bring papers over for you to sign."

"Me?"

"That's right. You're going to give me permission to entertain bids on the drive-in."

"I don't own the drive-in."

"Doesn't matter," says Chuck. "You're not selling it. You're just giving me permission to show it to potential buyers."

Billy stops eating the popcorn.

"Herb didn't say anything about selling the place."

Chuck's phone goes off like a bomb in his pocket. It's the general ring tone as opposed to the ring tone he gets when his secretary at the real estate office calls, and it's different from the long-distance calls he gets from time to time. This is a general call, someone in town, someone Chuck doesn't know.

The caller is a woman. She sounds as though she's talking in a bucket.

"There's a problem at the house on Manzanita."

And then whoever it is hangs up.

Chuck holds the phone for a moment, tries to make sense of the call. And then he remembers. He has a listing on Manzanita.

"Tomorrow," Chuck tells Billy. "I'll bring the papers by."

"You want me to sign for Herb."

"In a manner of speaking."

"What's in it for me?"

Chuck wants to kick Billy in the shins. "You can keep the pickup for the next couple of days."

"Two weeks."

"One week."

"Deal," says Billy.

CHUCK DISCOVERS THAT HE didn't have to climb the fence, finds that if he pushes on the gate, there's enough slack in the chain to let him slip through. Which he does with only minor damage to his shirt.

The call could be a hoax of some sort. The scams that are popping up every day are more and more sophisticated. Mostly they appear on the internet, warnings about your credit cards or your computer service. Amazon is a favourite ploy. Everyone has an Amazon account, and you can cause a stampede with a threat to a delivery.

But real estate has not been exempt. There have been a series of mortgage frauds that have totalled into the millions and have cost people their homes. As Chuck drives back into town, he replays the phone call in his head.

There's a problem at the house on Manzanita.

Curious. The caller didn't say there is a problem *with* the house on Manzanita. She said that the problem was *at* the house. And sure enough, when Chucks gets to the house on Manzanita, he can see the problem immediately.

His real estate sign is gone.

Do people have any idea what those things cost? Teenage delinquents. Having a good time. Let's go pull up real estate signs. That should be fun.

Chuck parks the car and gets out. Which is when he notices that not only is the sign gone, but the front door is cracked open.

Not good. Someone has broken in. He has been meaning to change the code on the lockbox.

He's halfway up the walk when he realizes that this is Nico's house. Or, more specifically, Nico's mother's house. Vandalized. Robbed. And Nico is sure to blame him.

Chuck stands at the front door.

"Hello?" He takes out his cellphone, holds it up. "I'm calling the police."

The house is quiet and dark. Maybe whoever broke in was disturbed and frightened, and the only damage is the missing sign and the open door. Chuck expects to find the TV missing and the place trashed, but there's no need to jump to conclusions until they need jumping.

"Hello?" Chuck turns on the cellphone's flashlight. It's a handy feature, but unnecessary. So far as he can remember, the power hasn't been turned off. He finds the light switch and flips it up.

And breathes a sigh of relief.

The place looks perfectly fine. No graffiti on the walls. No television ripped from its moorings. No food scattered about. No signs of rifling. All is calm, all is bright.

Except for the old woman slumped over on the sofa.

Chuck walks back to the car, sits behind the wheel, runs through his options. Okay. He puts a handkerchief over his mouth, calls the police. He doesn't give his name, just a general description of the situation.

"There's a problem at the house on Manzanita."

And then he drives away.

XVIII

Ellen Tidy takes a taxi home.

The affair with the police should have been devastating, humiliating, but Ellen found it exhilarating. Fingerprints, photo, the signing of forms. Overnight in a jail cell.

All that attention.

Just like in the true crime shows she likes to watch.

Ellen the Felon. Released on her own recognizance. Loosed on the world once again. The truck is in impound, and the police have made it clear that it isn't going to be returned anytime soon.

But that's okay. It's Gary's truck.

Brenda Price.

The Price is right.

Ellen doesn't know why she got so upset. If Gary wants to screw Brenda, that's Brenda's problem. In the meantime, Ellen is free. Sure, she's supposed to show up for a hearing, but she's already decided against doing that. What a waste of time. She'll be found guilty. She might even be sentenced to some jail time, ordered to make restitution to Walmart.

Ellen has seen the corporation's year-end profits. They sure as hell don't need any restitution.

Ellen drags a suitcase from the closet, packs her clothes. Just what she needs. Then she goes online and transfers the money from their current account to a new account that she opens in her name only.

Leaves Gary with enough to get him through the month. Which is more than he deserves.

Then she pulls up a map of Canada on the monitor, closes her eyes, sticks a finger on a spot. Oh, yes, that could be nice. Okay, she'll start there. A quick phone call to the airline, another to the airport shuttle. The rest she'll figure out as she goes.

Yes, it's all a little crazy, and yes, there's a good chance that this will end badly. When she doesn't show up for the hearing, the judge will issue a bench warrant. Ellen can't count the number of bench warrants she's seen issued on *Court Cam*.

But they don't scare her. With Gary and Autumn Leaves as the alternatives, how much does she really have to lose?

Pearson is busy. Ellen didn't realize the number of people on the move. How many are headed out for a holiday? How many are off visiting family? How many away for business?

How many are soon-to-be felons on the run?

Ellen shuffles her way to security with its plastic trays filled with belts and shoes and laptops. She waits her turn to go through the metal detector. She doesn't think they'll have her photograph on a watch list. It's too soon for that. But the episode at Walmart did make the internet. Any number of people took videos with their cellphones, posted the images of Ellen driving the truck up and down the aisles.

She's a bit of a YouTube celebrity.

Maybe one of the security guards will recognize her, ask her for an autograph.

For Jonas. Let's do it again. Best, Ellen.

THE PLANE IS DELAYED. Ellen sits in the waiting area, discovers that she is exhausted. All the stimulation has turned to exhaustion. And doubt. Is this a mistake? Should she stay and face the music? Reconcile with Gary? Show Brenda Price that she can't take Ellen's man?

Ewww. Just the thought is nauseating.

No. This is the right decision. Into the unknown. Maybe divine intervention will bless her voyage. Maybe an omen will come along, a psychic hint of some sort or other. But no matter what, when the plane lands, she'll be getting off and starting over.

With any luck, she'll get it right this time.

Darlene sleeps in late, doesn't get up until after ten. Billy didn't come home last night, so she doesn't have to deal with him wanting sex first thing in the morning. Darlene doesn't think that having sex in the morning is natural. She's watched enough nature shows to know that animals don't wake up from a sound sleep and jump on each other.

Darlene checks her money, just in case Billy *did* come in while she was sleeping and rob her. No, it's still where she put it. In her bra. It's a little damp, but it's all there.

Billy makes fun of her for having peanut butter on toast, but she's looked it up on the internet. Protein and carbohydrates. Every bit as good as ham and eggs. As she eats, she plans her day. Put gas in the car. Buy the weed she needs for the foreseeable future. Drive over to the woman's house, return the fanny pack, collect her reward.

Gross. Zoltan has done his business in the corner of the living room near the TV. On the carpet. That's because Billy forgot to let him out. Zoltan is his dog. He can clean up the mess.

Darlene puts the dirty dish in the sink with the other dirty dishes and walks out into the day.

Mrs. Thea Karras lives on Manzanita Avenue, across the street from a small park. The house is a low-slung bungalow. Clapboard or shiplap siding. Jackson would know the one from the other. If Darlene asks, her stepfather will give her a lecture on wood siding, which will make her feel stupid, so she isn't going to ask. It's a cute house. That's all that counts.

Darlene sits in her car and goes over what she's going to say.

Hi, I found your purse.

It was in the bathroom at the hospital.

I think someone went through it, because it was open.

And the wallet was on the floor.

No. That's too much information. If the wallet was on the floor, which it wasn't, Mrs. Karras will suppose that Darlene went through it as well. Just say that it was on the bathroom floor.

It was on the bathroom floor.

I was going to turn it in at the nurses' station.

But then I thought it would be better if I brought it to you personally.

Wait. How could Darlene know where to bring the purse unless she had gone through it? Which would raise the question of where the money went.

I'm afraid the money is gone.

This is harder than Darlene thought it would be. There's no way she could have known who the purse belonged to or where the owner lived unless she had gone through the purse. And if she tells Mrs. Karras that the money is gone, it means that Darlene knew there was money in the purse in the first place.

I found your purse in the hospital bathroom. I took all the money. I found your name and address on your hospital card. I'm returning the purse because I expect a reward.

The truth doesn't sound any better. Best to stick to the lie.

Darlene gets out of the car, walks up the walk to the front door.

Knock or press the doorbell? Knocking might seem rude. It might even startle an old lady. Darlene doesn't want to do that. She wants Mrs. Karras to be calm and friendly, wants her to see Darlene as a friend, a benefactor.

The doorbell makes a standard *ding-dong*. Darlene is disappointed. There are all sorts of doorbells that play tunes, but then she realizes that this is the old house of an old woman.

Nothing happens.

Darlene presses the doorbell again. She can hear the *ding-dong* distinctly, and unless Mrs. Karras is deaf, she can hear it, too. If she's home. Darlene hadn't considered the possibility that Mrs. Karras is off somewhere, in which case, she has made a trip for nothing.

But then she hears movement. Someone *is* home.

"Hellooooo." Darlene stretches the vowels out in a pleasant singsong manner to reassure the older woman that a friend is at the door. "Hellooooo."

More shuffling noises. Maybe Mrs. Karras has dementia. That might explain her reluctance to open the door.

"Mrs. Karras?"

Darlene hears the deadbolt retract. The door opens a crack, as far as the security chain will let it.

"Are you from Autumn Leaves?"

"I found your fanny pack."

"My son send you?"

"You left it in the bathroom." Darlene holds out the fanny pack, so Thea can see it. "At the hospital."

"My fanny pack?"

"That's right," says Darlene. "I found it."

Through the gap between the door and the frame, Darlene can see an eye now and part of a face. Mrs. Karras is older than she had imagined.

"Hi, I'm Darlene."

"I don't know you."

"That's right," says Darlene, "you don't."

"And you found my fanny pack."

"I did."

Darlene hears the security chain being removed.

"I suppose you should come in." Thea stands in the doorway, a rolling pin in one hand. Darlene's mother has one just like it. "But no funny stuff. I know karate."

It's a French rolling pin. Darlene's mother has explained the difference between rolling pins. Not that Darlene cares. People who worry about rolling pins are people who want to bake shit.

Darlene follows Thea into the living room. The furniture is old-person creepy. Dark wood chairs. Floral patterns in blues and yellows. All the curtains are closed. The place feels like a cave, and maybe this is how old people like to live. In the dark.

Thea sits in one of the ugly chairs and goes through her fanny pack. "What happened to my money?"

What do you think happened to your money, you old cow? I took it. I went through your fanny pack and I took all your money. I filled my gas tank, bought a bunch of weed, and the rest of your cash is in my pocket.

"No idea," says Darlene. "I guess someone found it before I did and took the money."

Thea sits in the chair like a large chicken, cocks her head. Looks at Darlene as though Darlene was a juicy worm.

"I had over three hundred dollars in my fanny pack."

It was only $265. And some change.

"That's terrible." Darlene makes her sad face. "I'm so sorry."

"How much is left?"

At first, Darlene doesn't understand the question.

"You took my money." Thea puts the rolling pin on her lap, keeps her voice flat. "How much is left?"

Jesus. Is the old cow a mind reader?

"I needed it." Darlene can't believe she says this.

Thea nods. "Of course you did."

"I didn't have any gas, and I need weed to help me sleep, and my boyfriend beat me up, and I was at the hospital."

Everything just spills out.

"My mom is always on me, and my stepdad hates me." Darlene has tears in her eyes. "And I have to buy food for the stupid dog."

"My son put me in a dump," says Thea. "Do you have any children?"

Oh my god. Darlene has forgotten about Jor-El. Her beautiful baby. She has to take a moment to remember where she left her son. Right. With her mother. Which is okay, because grandmothers love their grandchildren and grandchildren love their grandparents. Jor-El probably loves Jackson.

"I do," says Darlene. "Jor-El. He's five. He's so smart."

"Smarter than my son," says Thea. "That's for sure."

Darlene relaxes. The old woman isn't half bad. In fact, Darlene feels as though she's beginning to bond with Mrs. Karras.

"You want something? A glass of water? A soda?"

"What I want," says Thea, "is a daughter."

THEA HAS DARLENE GET the photo album from the bookshelf. They sit at the kitchen table and look at the pictures.

"That's me when I was young," says Thea. "All the boys wanted to buy me things."

"You were hot."

"And that's my husband. Never marry a good-looking man."

"I'm never getting married."

"And this is my son." Thea touches the picture with a finger. "He was a sweet boy."

"He is so cute."

"And then the *vlaka* grew up and married that *chazí gynaíka*."

"Do you have grandchildren?"

Thea's face is a storm cloud. "No," she says. "I have no grand-children."

Thea goes through the entire album. It's interesting, but it's not the way Darlene wants to spend her day.

Thea closes the album. "So, you stole my money."

Darlene waits.

"But you brought my fanny pack back."

"Health cards are hard to replace," says Darlene. "I know. My boyfriend sold mine, and it took a long time to get a new one."

"You expect a reward?"

Darlene can see the problem. She can't exactly expect a reward for stealing money.

Thea runs her hand along the rolling pin. "Have you ever been to African Lion Safari?"

THE DRIVE TO AFRICAN Lion Safari is a little over half an hour. Thea fills Darlene in as they drive.

"You have to stay away from the elephants," says Thea. "And the lions aren't much better."

Darlene doesn't plan to go anywhere near the lions.

"The trick is to stay in the car."

Darlene has no intention of getting out.

"And the baboons can be pretty destructive."

DARLENE HADN'T KNOWN WHAT to expect, but African Lion Safari was great. She was sorry that she didn't have Jor-El with her instead of Mrs. Karras. Maybe once she gets a job and has some extra money, she'll bring her son to the game park.

That was the downside. The cost. Admission was over forty dollars. Which meant eighty dollars for two people. That just about took the rest of the money that Darlene had. Sure, it was Mrs. Karras's money, but now that it was in Darlene's pocket, it felt like hers.

On the way home, Thea goes to sleep. Which is just as well. The old woman likes to talk about her son and how badly he treats her, and when she starts in, she reminds Darlene of her own mother.

It's heading for evening when they get back to Thea's house.

"You should eat something," says Thea. "There are frozen dinners in the freezer."

Darlene doesn't want to stick around. Yes, Mrs. Karras has been fun, and the old woman hasn't given her a hard time for taking her money, but she is old and Darlene has things to do and places to go.

"I know how to make those," says Darlene.

"A daughter would take care of me," says Thea. "That's why I wanted one."

DARLENE HAS HER CHOICE between fettucine Alfredo, beef bourguignon, and chicken Parmesan. She opts for the chicken Parmesan. Thea has the bourguignon. They sit at the kitchen table and watch a reality show about love at first sight.

"My friend Joan likes to watch this show," says Thea. "She thinks it's real."

Darlene isn't sure that it's not.

"She's not really a friend," says Thea, "but when you get to be my age, you take what you can get."

"You see the girl in the shorts? And the guy with the muscular stomach?" Darlene waves a fork at the television. "He's trying to get into her pants."

Thea pushes away from the table, goes to the living room, arranges herself on her sofa.

"At seven, it's *Murder, She Wrote.*"

Darlene has seen parts of the show. It's really old and the stories are mostly stupid and there are no special effects.

"They're reruns," says Thea, "but I still enjoy them."

The chicken Parmesan is nothing to write home about. The noodles are tasteless and the chicken is tough and dried out. Still, it's food. And she didn't have to pay for it.

"Where's the bathroom?"

"End of the hall," says Thea. "Last left. Make sure to leave the lid down on the toilet."

Darlene's mother tells her the same thing. As though an open toilet is an affront to god.

"And don't use too much toilet paper."

The bathroom is small and done up in pink and green tile with the fixtures in harvest yellow. The bathroom at Jackson's house is white and green tiles with green fixtures. Darlene figures the two houses were built around the same time.

Way before cellphones.

Darlene sits on the toilet and tries to think of a way to bring the conversation around to her reward for returning the fanny pack. She can't sit here all night, and she's beginning to think that she's going to have to leave empty-handed. Mrs. Karras has been nice enough, and if Darlene had a grandmother, she'd want her to be like Thea.

But the tickets for African Lion Safari were expensive, and now she doesn't have much money left and has no idea where she might get some more.

Darlene finishes with the toilet, washes her hands, notices the medicine cabinet with the mirror. Jackson has a similar medicine cabinet, so Darlene knows that the mirror is actually a door and that it swings out. Maybe Mrs. Karras has some Oxy or some other medication that she can sell. She won't take all of it, just enough to make up for the gas she used to get to the safari place and back.

The cabinet is bare. Nothing. Not even aspirin. Darlene checks the drawers, just in case. Nothing.

Well, she did steal the woman's money. Maybe this is cosmic payback. Maybe the aliens on the moon are laughing at her right now.

ANGELA LANSBURY IS ON the television. She's talking with Doc Hazlitt. Mrs. Karras is sitting on the sofa. Her eyes are closed. Probably bored to death by old TV shows. Darlene thinks about searching the house for something to sell. After all, there *should* be a reward for returning the fanny pack.

"Hey, Mrs. K," says Darlene, "I have to get going. You going to be okay?"

Nothing.

"I can come back tomorrow, if you like." Darlene sits down next to Mrs. Karras, takes the remote control out of her hand. "But I'm going to need money for gas."

Nothing.

Darlene waves a hand in front of Thea's face. "Hey, you still alive?"

ria certainly isn't going to work at the Blue Bird Café the rest of her life. That's for damn sure. Split shift, double shift. Coming home smelling like liver and onions. In the fall, she's heading off to university. Say goodbye to the good times.

Taking people's orders.

"No, you can't substitute the salad for fries."

Complaints about the size of the portions.

"I'm sure we can make them smaller."

Food that's not hot enough.

"Let's see if we can make the soup bubble and pop."

And university will get her out of the house once and for all. It's not that she doesn't like her parents and her grandmother, but they're her parents and her grandmother, and they all want to tell her what to do.

"Don't want you to make the same mistakes I made," her mother tells her.

What mistakes are those? Bria wants to know.

"You don't want to know," her father says.

Bria's grandmother joins in. "Listen to your mother. Listen to your father."

"The plan is to go to university," Bria told the family. "Become a doctor. Go to some developing country. Save sick kids."

"Universities cost money," said her mother. "Those places are for rich white kids."

"You know how racist that sounds?"

"You're not a rich white kid."

"Northern Manitoba," said Bria's grandmother. "They could use that kind of help in Northern Manitoba."

"Or I could shack up with some bum, get hooked on drugs, get knocked up, die in a gutter."

Her mother makes a face each time Bria says this, so she says it often. Her life. Her mistakes.

The latest mistake was the rosary. She should never have listened to her grandmother, who has made the matter worse by telling everyone on the reserve about the rosary and the Pope.

"You're a hero," her grandmother tells her.

"I have a shift at the café."

"Good job like that," says her grandmother, "why do you want to run off to Montreal?"

"Kingston."

BRIA GETS TO THE café on time. She won't miss the smell of bacon and coffee. She won't miss stingy customers. She won't miss the stupid T-shirt that Arnold makes everyone wear.

Blue Bird Café. Blue shirt. Gold letters. Bria always feels like a high school cheerleader when she puts it on.

The café is almost empty, but it will pick up closer to lunch. Bria recognizes most of the patrons. Cafés such as the Blue Bird have a squad of irregulars, who make the place feel like a dysfunctional family.

Today, Chuck Mason and Jackson Mosley are huddled together in a corner booth. Bria has seen Mason's real estate signs around town.

Save a Buck, Talk to Chuck.

Chuck can go to Wendy's for all Bria cares. Always leaves a dollar. Rain or shine. Jackson is okay. Bria isn't sure what he does for a living, but he's friendly. And he tips.

The Cusano sisters are at their usual table. Soup and dinner buns with a salad that they split. Save room for the pie.

Martin Slocum is at the counter, nursing a coffee and a bran muffin.

Mr. and Mrs. Albright are in the window, watching the world go by over hot roast beef sandwiches, letting the world watch them.

Bria will not miss the Blue Bird one little bit. If she thought that this is all life has to offer, she'd grab a knife from the kitchen and slit her wrists. Maybe the aliens will abduct her. Life aboard a spaceship couldn't be any more boring than this.

"Scuse me." Chuck holds his coffee cup up, waggles it as though it's a bell.

Bria grabs the pot, slaps on a smile. Gotta earn that dollar.

"Hi, Bria. Hear you're off to university." Mr. Mosley has a pleasant face. "Congratulations."

Why Mr. Mosley and Mr. Mason are friends is a mystery. But today, they don't seem too friendly. As Bria goes back to the counter, she hears Chuck's voice snap.

"What the hell was I supposed to do?"

"You should have called the police."

"I did."

"You should have stuck around."

"Forget the old lady," says Chuck. "How about we get back to your inflated invoice."

"It's not inflated," says Jackson. "You signed off on all the changes."

"Yeah, well, we need to renegotiate."

"I've already bought the materials."

"So, take the difference out of the labour end."

"You mean out of *my* end."

"Come on, Jackson." Chuck sits back in the booth. "You gotta meet me halfway."

Bria thinks about going back to the table and pouring hot coffee on Mr. Mason's lap. Just the thought cheers her up. Or maybe she'll fish the rosary out of the cheese box. If she can hit the Pope from across a couple of provinces, she sure as hell can nail Chuck Mason across a café.

Good enough for the Holy Father, good enough for One Buck Chuck.

Instead, she puts the orders in. A BLT for Mr. Mosley, hold the mayo. A Monte Cristo with fries for Mr. Mason, may the cholesterol clog his arteries. There are days when she feels like taking off the stupid Blue Bird Café T-shirt, stripping down to her bra and the girls, and walking away from the soup du jours and the luncheon specials.

And do what?

Go to university? Sure, that's what she tells her parents. What she tells her grandmother. And maybe she will. Someday. But first, she needs to get out of the house. She won't figure out life staying at home. Home is a time-free zone. No one grows up. No one grows old. Nothing changes, nothing moves ahead.

University is the excuse for leaving, the easy way to escape. No hurt feelings. Her father wants to drive her to Kingston, wants to help her get settled. Hell, her mother and grandmother want to come along as well. Bria has had to work hard to murder that idea.

"I need to do this on my own."

"Sure," her father tells her, "I'll just do the driving."

"I can catch the train."

Her grandmother is predictable. "By yourself?"

Her mother more supporting. "Of course, by herself."

"You ran away when you were her age." Bria's grandmother's memory is a razor. "And look what happened."

"What happened?"

Bria's mother with her face set. "None of your business, young lady."

In the end, everyone agrees that the train is a good solution, and that university is a good solution, and there is no discussion as to what either will solve.

But she's not going to university, is she? She'd need money for that. And she's not going to Kingston. And she sure as hell isn't going to work at the Blue Bird any longer than necessary.

"Hey, girl." Tabby Marcotte slides onto a stool at the counter. "I need a drink."

Bria smiles. Tabby makes her laugh, brightens a Blue-Bird, One-Buck-Chuck day.

"Coffee?"

"Beer," says Tabby. "And a baseball bat."

"How about a milkshake?"

"Vanilla."

"Can't help you with the bat."

Tabby turns on the stool. "Just as well I don't have a bat. I'd take out her kneecaps."

Bria waits.

"Boss lady at Autumn Leaves," says Tabby. "Bitch fired me."

"Fired you?"

"Took the old cows to the mall for their Saturday treat." Tabby picks at the napkin dispenser. "End of the day, the bus breaks down, and we're running around trying to figure out what to do, and in the end, we have to get a bunch of taxis to take us all back to Autumn Leaves."

"Who'd you lose?"

"Didn't lose anyone," says Tabby. "Not my fault Karras can't follow directions."

"Karras? Mrs. Karras?"

"Yeah," says Tabby. "You know her?"

"She was in here Saturday," says Bria.

"In here?" says Tabby. "On Saturday?"

"Late afternoon," says Bria. "Her son just died. Pretty sad."

"Well, guess what?" Tabby leans in. "She's dead as well."

"Mrs. Karras?"

Tabby nods. "Boss lady's been on the phone all day with the police and with Karras's son."

"Her son's dead."

"Maybe she has more than one." Tabby takes a deep breath, lets it out. "Anyway, that's how I got fired."

BRIA FINISHES HER SHIFT. Twenty dollars and fifty cents in tips. Which she has to split with the kitchen. Hardly worth the effort. Probably would make more panhandling in front of the ATM on Wyndham. Maybe she and Tabby should take off together. Not Kingston and sure as hell not Toronto. Maybe Halifax, except the winters are shit. Maybe west. Manitoba. Saskatchewan. Alberta. Bet they have good-paying jobs in Alberta. Maybe even all the way to the west coast.

Somewhere other than here.

BRIA'S GRANDMOTHER IS ON the sofa. Her mother and father are sitting at the kitchen table.

"Did you hear?" says her grandmother. "The aliens have blown up the Vatican."

Bria's father waves a finger in the air. "Kitchen fire. Got out of hand."

"Some kind of death ray," says her grandmother. "Like a lightning bolt. They have video."

"Maybe the Pope can wave a rosary around," says Bria. "Scare them off."

"That's nothing to joke about, young lady," says her mother.

"How's work?" asks her father.

"I should be selling drugs."

"That's nothing to joke about." Bria's mother straightens the placemat. "Look what happened to your cousin."

"The one who owns the marijuana outlet on the reserve? The one with the Audi convertible?"

"He's not happy," says Bria's mother, "I can tell you that."

"Tabby got fired," says Bria. "From the old folks' home."

"That might be a good job."

"Dad, I'm not taking Tabby's job."

"You said she got fired."

"Besides, I'm going to university."

Bria's father nods. "I'm thinking you just want to get out of the house."

"You want to get out of the house," says her grandmother, "do what all the girls do."

"I'm not getting married."

"Getting married and raising children is a good job."

"Ewww."

"Why would you want to get out of the house?" asks Bria's mother.

"Duh," says Bria's father. "To get away from us. That's what all kids want to do."

B RIA SPENDS THE REST of the evening in her room watching Hospice Nurse Julie videos on her phone. First thing the next morning, she calls Tabby.

"Hey."

"Wassup."

"Nada."

"Double nada."

"You want to do something?"

"Like?"

"Move to Alberta. Get a job in the tar sands."

"My bags are packed."

"I'm serious."

"Café hiring?" asks Tabby.

"You want my job?" says Bria. "You can have my job."

L UNCH IS BUSY. T HE couple who are planning a fourteen-day cruise to the Caribbean. A young man on his cellphone arguing with a girlfriend. A mother making silly noises at a baby in a stroller. Two business types, full of themselves, intent on owning the world.

Bria floats through the café, pouring coffee, taking orders, catching snatches of conversation, making small talk with the regulars.

And when her shift is over, she goes home.

The flight from Toronto to Calgary is four hours and fifteen minutes. Unless, as Herb discovers, you fly Air Canada. Yes, there's the two hours prior to the flight that he has to endure, as well as the ticket machines in the main concourse with their Out of Order signs and the *1984* security check that has him doing a slow strip sans music.

Belt, glasses, hat, shoes. Everything in his pockets. Stray thoughts.

His carry-on is placed in a plastic tray and whisked away into the throat of the X-ray machine. He has to walk through a portal where he's blasted with god-knows-what, which will show up shortly as something terminal.

The whole process is mechanical and soulless. Even though Herb does not believe in souls.

After which he is spat out into the airport shopping mall replete with everything Herb does not need or want. He thinks about getting something for Leroy.

A Blue Jays baseball cap?

An "I Love Toronto" T-shirt?

Herb slaps himself mentally. *Grow up.*

There are handy screens strategically placed along the concourse that tell Herb where and when his flight is to board. Except it's been delayed by half an hour. An Air Canada half-hour. Which is somewhat longer than a normal half-hour.

By the time Herb gets on the plane, the flight is over three hours late. His seat is at the very back. There are three groups of three seats. Left, centre, right. Herb finds himself in the middle seat in the centre group.

"Almost criminal, ain't it?"

The man next to him isn't fat, but he is large, and parts of him push over onto Herb's armrest.

"Old days, the seats were made for people," says the man. "Now, they're made for pipe cleaners."

Herb agrees that the seats are small.

"I'm Bob," says the man. "Bob Porter."

"Herb Good Runner," says Herb. "Retired."

"That's the job I want," says Bob.

The man on the other side of Herb is also large. Herb sits in his tiny seat, hemmed in on both sides, blocked front and back, and begins to regret his decision. And as the aircraft begins the taxi to the end of the runway, Herb wonders if there is still time to get off the plane.

"First time flying?" asks Bob. "I only mention it because you seem a little nervous."

"No," says Herb. "I've flown before. But it's been a while."

"Back when we used to get a movie?"

"There's no movie?"

Bob chuckles. "Those times are long gone."

"Is there a meal?"

"Welcome to the Air Canada Bistro." Bob takes a brochure out of the seat pocket, hands it to Herb. "Coffee and tea are still free."

The brochure has a menu. With prices. Cold sandwiches. A couple of hot meals.

"The stuff's no worse than what you get at Timmies," says Bob. "And no better."

The seat is more uncomfortable than Herb would have imagined. The seat cushion is thin, and the back curves in at an angle that hurts his neck. He can't imagine anyone sitting this way for four hours.

"Now, if you were in business class," says Bob, "you'd get a pretty nice meal as part of the package. Last year, I flew business class on points. Toronto to Vancouver. Had a lie-down seat." Bob makes a low whistle. "That was sweet. Could turn the seat into a bed. Pillows and a comforter. Had your own TV with a bunch of movies. And if you wanted anything, you just pushed a button."

Bob's daughter teaches at the University of British Columbia.

"Religious studies," says Bob. "If you would believe it. And she's not even religious. Comparative stuff. History of this and that. You know which city in Canada is the least religious?"

Herb has no idea.

"Nanaimo," says Bob. "Quebec City is supposedly the holiest city, and southern Alberta is Canada's Bible Belt. Oldest religion? Hinduism. Fastest growing religion? Islam. You hear about the aliens landing out by Cardston?"

Herb nods. "On the Blackfoot reserve."

"That's right. Kady, that's my daughter—Kady is pretty sure you're going to see a bunch of new religious movements pop up. Aliens land on the moon and, bam, some hockey puck is going to start hearing voices, or he'll find an alien artifact buried in a field, or he'll get transported up to the mother ship for a short course in alien theology."

Herb smiles. Tries to find the button to recline the seat.

"I'll talk your ear off if you let me," says Bob. "You married?"

Herb nods.

"Kids?"

"Twins," says Herb. "Nathaniel and Abigail."

"Family," says Bob. "In the end, they're all you got."

By the time the plane lands in Calgary, Herb has confirmed the obvious. That packing this many sweaty people into this small a space is inexcusable. And after four hours of forcible confinement and having to breathe through his mouth, he's not sure he can pull himself out of the seat in one go.

"You need help?" Bob asks Herb. "Sardines in a can got more room."

It's a long walk to the main concourse. Herb starts off limping, his hip aching, his back and neck stiff and rigid, but as he moves, his body begins to loosen up. By the time he gets to the car rental desk, he's worked out most of the kinks.

"Hi," says the young woman, "how can Budget help you today?"

"I'd like to rent a car."

"Do you have a reservation?"

Herb toys with the old joke. *In Canada, we call it a reserve.* Decides against it. He's tired. Just wants to get on the road.

"No," he says. "No reservation."

"I'm sorry," says the woman. "But we don't have any cars available."

"No cars?"

"Calgary Stampede," says the woman. "And then there's that alien ship out near Lethbridge."

"No cars at all?"

The woman shakes her head. "None of the rental agencies have cars. Hope you have a hotel reservation."

"Is there a bus?"

"A bus?"

"To Lethbridge."

The woman might be twenty-two or she could be sixteen. "You could fly."

THE BENCH IN THE airport is wood. An artistic creation made of individual slats that have been steamed and bent. Herb settles in against the curves, his bag on his lap, closes his eyes.

Okay, what to do now?

He could call Leroy. His cousin would come to Calgary and pick him up. Or he could fly to Lethbridge. Rent a car at the airport, drive to the reserve. And if he doesn't want to stay on the reserve, he could get a room at the Lethbridge Lodge. He and Katherine stayed there for his mother's funeral.

So, why is he here? After all the years, why has he come back? Or maybe the better question is why did he leave? Lots of good excuses. The blisteringly hot summers. The winters that sucked the moisture out of your body. The politics that left you breathless.

But no good reasons in the lot.

He had just left.

Left family and friends. Left a magical landscape of prairies and mountains, the long run of the horizon, the curve of the sky. Left an ancient world of songs and stories.

Not enough. It hadn't been enough to hold him.

AND NOW HE IS back. Back on a bench in the Calgary airport, a carry-on bag on his lap. Full circle.

Across the concourse is a restaurant with a large television on the wall. From where he is sitting, Herb can see a red Breaking News banner on the screen. He gets off the bench, joins a small group of people who gather to watch what a reporter is calling "the unfolding drama."

Altercation on the Blood reserve. Police on site. Suspects in custody.

More people arrive, and the group begins to quiver with energy.

"It's the aliens," says a woman. "I knew this was going to happen."

"Someone tried to run the blockade."

"Anybody dead?"

"It's beginning. No stopping it now."

"*Predator*. It's just like *Predator*."

Like standing in a herd of cattle. In a lightning storm. Herb makes his way out of the murmuring crowd. Worse than being on the plane. Makes his way back to the bench. He should call Leroy, find out what's happening. But then he'd have to tell his cousin that he's in Calgary.

An irony, for sure.

To come all this way and now he's not sure he wants to go any farther. What is there for me on the reserve? A couple of people. Handful of memories. A remembered landscape. Fragments of a lost life.

What he should do is catch a flight back to Toronto, go back to the life he had at the drive-in, watching westerns, hitting golf balls against the screen. Which, if he's being honest, isn't much of a life.

Go home or go home. These are the choices.

Except there is no home. Home died with Katherine and the twins. So, for now, he'll sit on the bench, watch people pass by on their way to someplace else.

Been here long enough.

Later, he'll have dinner across the way at the restaurant with the TV, follow the news, as though he's right there with his cousin on the front lines. And after that, he'll wander the concourse, buy a book to read, pick up an "I Love Calgary" T-shirt for the hell of it.

And then he'll come back to the bench, sit and wait for the world to end.

As it has, each and every day. For as long as he can remember.

illy has to admit that the snack bar looks a lot better now that Darlene has decorated it. The toaster is a welcome addition, and the stained-glass lamp warms the bedroom area.

Better yet, Darlene has brought a shitload of frozen dinners that they can just toss into the microwave. Along with a health card and a social insurance card that he can sell.

"You didn't hang on to the purse, did you?"

"Course not. You think I'm stupid?"

"But no cash."

Darlene keeps her face flat. "Nope. No cash."

Billy walks around the snack bar, touching things as he goes. "So, what do you think?"

"The old guy just gave this to you?"

"That's right. I'm sort of the property manager."

"And we can live here?"

"Beats having to put up with your asshole stepfather and his house." Billy pulls the gun out of his pants, aims it at the popcorn machine. "Now, I'm the boss."

"OMG."

"What?"

"Jor-El." Darlene starts to tear up. "We forgot Jor-El."

"Relax," says Billy. "Your folks are looking after him."

"Yeah," says Darlene, "but he should be with his mother."

"Not happening."

"What do you mean?"

Billy puts the gun on the counter. "We got a good thing going. Me. You. The drive-in. No one to tell us what to do. Why do you want the kid to mess things up?"

"He's my child. I can't just leave him with my parents."

"Sure you can. He's happy where he is. They take good care of him."

"You're mean."

"Hey, this is my place."

"It's not your place. It's Mr. Fine Runner's."

"Good Runner," says Billy. "But he's not here. So, I'm in charge."

Darlene takes a quick step forward and snatches the gun off the counter, points it at Billy.

"Now, who's in charge?"

Billy's smiling. "Jesus, you are a stupid bitch."

Darlene cocks the gun.

"That's a starter's pistol. It's loaded with blanks. You can shoot me all you want and it's not going to do anything."

"Jor-El lives with us," she says. "Say it or I'll shoot you."

Billy holds his arms out. "Shoot away."

Darlene pulls the trigger.

DARLENE DOESN'T REMEMBER THE sequence of events. Not exactly. She remembers the gun in her hand. She remembers cocking the pistol. She remembers pulling the trigger, remembers being surprised by the loud report. Remembers Billy's ear.

And the screaming. She certainly remembers the screaming. All the way to the hospital.

"It was a starter's pistol," Darlene tells the doctor. "He said they weren't dangerous."

THE DOCTOR TAKES DARLENE off to one side.

"I've given your husband a sedative. He's a lucky man. A little to the right and he could have lost an eye. Maybe worse."

Darlene uses the bathroom. As she sits on the toilet, she realizes that this is how it all started. In a bathroom. The purse. If she hadn't found the purse and been a good Samaritan, she wouldn't have met Mrs. Karras. And if she hadn't met Mrs. Karras, she wouldn't have gone to the old woman's house. And maybe the old woman wouldn't have died.

You never know.

For sure, she wouldn't have taken the toaster and the frozen dinners and the lamp and Mrs. Karras's health card and her social insurance card. But as she goes through the chain of events, she realizes that what has happened is Billy's fault.

Billy found the gun. Billy told her that the thing was loaded with blanks. It was Billy who bad-mouthed her son and got her all angry. And it was Billy who told her to shoot him.

Not her fault. Not her fault. Not her fault.

Darlene finishes up, washes her hands, looks around the room in case someone else has left a purse or a wallet or a cellphone. You never know.

THERE ARE TWO POLICE officers waiting for her when she gets back to Billy's room. A man and a woman.

"I'm Constable Virone," says the woman. "And this is Constable Souto."

Darlene tries to remember if Billy has any drugs on him.

"Are you Mrs. Kiddle?"

Darlene is sure that there is a right answer, but she doesn't know what it is.

"Could you take us through what happened," says Souto.

Billy's pale. And he looks really old. Maybe that's what happens when you get shot and lose a lot of blood. The whole side of his head is bandaged. He's not going to be happy when he wakes up.

"Maybe start with who had the gun."

For the next hour, the two officers make Darlene tell the story over and over again. She tries to keep the story straight in her head, but each time they make her stop to explain something, she loses her place.

"So, Mr. Kiddle had the gun."

"That's right."

"Where did he get it?"

"Dunno."

"And he gave it to you?"

"That's right."

"Why did he do that?" asks Virone.

"Dunno."

"And then he asked you to shoot him?" Souto has a small smile on his face, the same kind of smile that her stepfather gets when he knows she's lying.

"He said the gun was safe, that it was a starter's pistol, that it was loaded with blanks."

"Blanks have wadding," says Virone. "At close range, the discharge can be as dangerous as a bullet."

Darlene remembers Billy's ear exploding.

"So, it was a game?"

"I guess."

"So, you weren't trying to kill him."

"I think the aliens made him do it." Darlene feels as though she might throw up. "He's been having these headaches."

"Headaches?"

This is the only thing that Darlene can remember from all the space movies she's seen. This is the only thing she can think of to say.

"Like someone was in there."

"In his head?"

"Yeah."

"Maybe you and the aliens were angry with Mr. Kiddle," says Virone.

Souto takes out his cellphone, scrolls through with his thumb. "Here's a domestic violence complaint that you filed against Mr. Kiddle in January. Is that what happened last night?"

Darlene can see that answering questions is not a good idea.

"And the gun," says Virone. "What happened to the gun?"

"Can I go home?" asks Darlene. "I'm hungry, and I don't feel good."

"Just a few more questions," says Virone.

"Is he going to die?"

BILLY IS DISCHARGED LATER that day. He's groggy from the drugs, but he's also angry.

"You shot me."

"You told me to shoot you."

"You see what you did to my ear?"

When they get back to the drive-in, Darlene turns on the popcorn machine. Billy flops on the sofa, moaning about his ear and how his head hurts. Darlene is sympathetic. And then she isn't.

"You don't love me."

"Hey, this isn't about you."

"You don't love Jor-El."

"Your kid's a brat."

"No, he's not."

"Can you just shut up and find me some painkillers?"

"Do I say anything about your stupid dog taking a shit on the carpet?"

"Hope to hell you fed him." Billy pulls his knees up against his chest, curls into a tight ball. "And where's my gun?"

Darlene sits in the recliner and listens to Billy complain. Everything is Darlene's fault. The gun, his ear, her son, his life. By the time he finally falls asleep, she realizes that he doesn't love her.

Well, she doesn't love him. And she doesn't need him. And she's sorry she didn't blow his head off. She actually thinks about doing just that, except she can't find the gun, and having to clean up all the blood would not be pleasant.

But enough is enough.

She quietly gathers up the toaster and the lamp, finds Mrs. Karras's cards, loads all the frozen dinners into the car and leaves.

Just like the aliens. Poof. Gone. Good enough for them, good enough for her.

Tomorrow, she'll figure out what to do next.

The funeral is a small affair, hardly a funeral at all. More a remembrance, and not even that.

"Your mother wasn't one for sentiment," Sudi tells Nico, by way of condolence. "She wouldn't have wanted anyone to make a fuss."

"She wanted a daughter," says Nico. "As if that would have made a difference."

"It was the police," says Sudi. "They kept the body for far too long."

Which was true. Almost a month passed before the body was released. As it was an unattended death, there was an autopsy, which was inconclusive.

And then there were the questions.

Why was an old woman in the house alone?

Why were there two sets of dirty dishes in the sink?

Who was the young woman the neighbours saw on the day of Karras's death?

And then there were the missing items. Thea's purse, for example. At first, Nico thought his mother had left it at Autumn Leaves, but it hadn't turned up there. He also recalled a toaster that had been plugged in next to the stove. And a faux Tiffany table lamp.

Anything else? the police had wanted to know.

Frozen dinners. Nico was sure there had been frozen dinners in the refrigerator's freezer.

In the time it took for the matter to plod its way to a conclusion—death by natural causes—the shock of his mother's death had worn off, and there was nothing left for Nico to do but arrange for a coffin and a burial.

"Why do we need a coffin?"

"We all need a coffin," the funeral director explained.

"How about a cardboard box?"

"They're only used in cremations."

"Are cremations cheaper than burials?"

Sudi stood by Nico through the entire process, explained to the funeral director that his mother's death had hit her husband hard, and that allowances should be made for the effects of grief.

"She wanted a daughter," Nico explained to the funeral director.

"Yes," said the funeral director. "I understand."

"She died at home," Sudi offered. "It's where she wanted to be."

Which complicated the property, in terms of a quick sale.

Chuck and Nico have coffee at the Blue Bird Café. He comes straight to the point. "No one wants to buy a death house."

"So, don't tell anyone."

"No can do, Nico," says Chuck. "Full disclosure. Asbestos, aluminum wiring, leaky basements, urea formaldehyde, rodent infestation, dead bodies."

"Rodent infestation?"

"We could try lowering the price. The aliens aren't helping. After the attack on the Vatican, everyone's hunkering down."

"The attack on the Vatican was a kitchen fire."

"That's the official story, all right." Chuck touches the side of his nose. "It wouldn't hurt to spruce the place up a little. Paint. Carpet. I can call Jackson, see if he's free."

Nico sits and stares at the table. Chuck leans back in his chair, waggles his coffee in the air as though he were ringing a bell.

"Little service here."

Nico doesn't notice the young woman until she's standing next to him.

"Aren't you Mrs. Karras's son?"

Nico looks up. He recognizes the waitress. Linda, Lucy, Lilly.

"Bria," says the young woman. "You and your mother used to come in here."

Nico smiles. "That's right."

Bria fills his cup. "We heard you were dead."

By the time Nico gets home, he's considering suing Autumn Leaves for losing his mother.

"They lose her, and she winds up dead."

"Not worth the time and trouble," Sudi tells him. "No one knows exactly what happened. Did she wander away? How did she get back to her house? Who was the mysterious young woman?"

"They shouldn't have lost her."

Sudi shows Nico a site on her computer that offers luxury ocean cruises. "Let's just concentrate on getting the house sold. We can use part of the money for a vacation."

Nico has to admit that the sparkling white ships do look splendid against the dark ocean and the bright blue sky. There's a young couple standing at the railing. The man's shirt is open. You can see his flat, hard stomach. The woman is wearing a tiny bikini that barely contains her soft parts. They hold champagne flutes in their hands, as the wind blows through their hair.

"That could be us." Sudi pushes her breasts up. "We could be that couple."

Nico sucks in his stomach. Unbuttons his shirt halfway down. "We are that couple."

Sudi pats his stomach. "Speaking of which, I heard from my sister."

"I know," says Nico, "she's changed her name again."

"Nope," says Sudi, "but the wedding is off."

"Tragic."

"As is CLAN."

"There goes our investment in the future."

"We shouldn't enjoy this," says Sudi.

"We'd be fools not to," says Nico.

THE NEXT MORNING AND the Subaru won't start. Gary Tidy is waiting for him when he gets to the dealership.

"*If it weren't for bad luck,*" Gary sings, "*you'd have no luck at all.*"

"So, you didn't get fired."

"Keep your voice down."

"What happened?"

"Nothing happened." Gary looks over Nico's shoulder. "Brenda left. Got a better job."

"They fired *her*?"

Gary gestures to the TV in the lounge. "Did you see the news?"

"The aliens?"

"You believe it?" says Gary. "They come all this way, plop down on the moon, send a scout expedition to Alberta, and then they just leave?"

"The spaceship is gone?"

"Left late last night," says Gary. "So, now we can all get back to normal."

"Maybe we can fix my car." Nico leans on the counter. "My *new* car."

"Chuck sell the house yet?" says Gary.

Nico shakes his head. "Not yet."

"I might be interested in renting," says Gary.

Aliens Give Up on Invasion is the banner headline on the TV.

"My lawyer says Ellen'll probably get the house. And the truck. You believe that?"

Nico wants to remind Gary that he was the one who had the affair.

"I mean, who stole my truck in the first place?" Gary's voice starts to crack. "And now the cops have my truck in impound, and I have to drive a rental."

Nico wants to mention the concept of poetic justice. But doesn't.

"A Nissan Murano. You believe that? A Nissan Murano!"

On the TV, there is a montage of military images. Clips of planes and tanks, missiles rising off their launching pads, aircraft carriers at sea, armies walking in formation. Second World War footage of Hiroshima and Nagasaki being destroyed.

"I mean, I didn't drive into Walmart with a snowplow and bust up the joint."

Nico wonders if the images are meant as a final warning to the aliens, in case they decide to return. Or a reminder of what we can do to ourselves.

"She's the felon."

Either way, it's effective.

"Chuck and Jackson are confirmed for Tuesday," says Gary. "You going to be able to make it?"

"My car?"

"You think we frightened the aliens away, like they say?" Gary takes Nico's keys, hangs them on a rack behind the counter. "Or maybe we just weren't worth their time."

Sᴜᴅɪ ɪs ɪɴ ᴛʜᴇ backyard at the patio table with an espresso and a book.

"Get the car fixed?"

"They're keeping it for a couple of days." Nico pulls up a chair.

"Rental?"

"Rental."

"The carpenter bees have been busy."

Sudi points to the bedroom window. There are long streaks of yellow-brown bee shit running down the glass.

"We just may have to learn to live with them."

Nico sighs, closes his eyes.

"At least the aliens are gone."

"You think my mother loved me?"

"Of course she did," says Sudi. "All mothers love their children."

"Filicide," says Nico. "It's not just a word."

Sudi puts the book to one side. "Sounds like someone needs a vacation. Where do you want to go?"

Nico smiles. "How about the moon?"

THAT NIGHT, NICO CAN'T sleep. He wanders around the living room, and then he goes out to the backyard, stands in the dark, looks at the moon. The aliens come all this way, and then they leave without a word.

Nico doesn't know what to make of that, but maybe now Subaru can fix the battery problem once and for all.

XXIV

Jill is reading to Jor-El. As soon as Jackson comes into the room, the little boy tumbles off the sofa and wraps himself around Jackson's leg.

"Pop-Pop-Pop-Pop-Pop-Pop."

Jackson picks him up and tosses him into the air, catches him, tosses him again.

Jill makes a face. "I wish you wouldn't do that."

"He likes it."

"He'd probably like it if you threw him off a cliff."

Jackson waits. "Darlene coming by to pick him up anytime soon?"

"I don't mind," says Jill. "It's nice having a baby in the house."

"He's not a baby." Jackson swings Jor-El back and forth. "And he has a mother."

"We need to talk about that."

Jackson drops Jor-El on the sofa. "What now?"

Jill rolls Jor-El onto her lap, gives him a long cuddle. "I'd like you to be a little flexible."

"I am flexible."

"And I don't want you to get angry."

"Why would I get angry?"

Jill lowers her voice. "Darlene has been arrested."

Jackson wanders into the kitchen, opens the refrigerator, takes out the bottle of lemonade syrup that's made by a company in Fergus.

"Did you hear me?"

Jackson pours a little of the syrup into a glass, fills it with water, throws in a few ice cubes.

"I hear you."

"And you're angry."

"I'm not angry."

"You sound angry. You don't want to upset Jor-El."

"Button," says Jackson. "Jor-El is a really dum—"

"Little ears." Jill's voice is a lilting singsong. "Little ears."

Jackson brings the glass to the sofa, sits down next to his wife and grandson.

"Let me know when you're calm."

Jackson takes a sip of the lemonade. He gives Button a sip. "All calm."

"Should we start with why she's been arrested?"

"Yes," says Jackson. "Why don't we start there."

Jill rubs Button's head. "Or should we feed Pop-Pop first?"

"Feed Pop-Pop," says Button. "Feed Pop-Pop."

DINNER IS POT ROAST. Carrots, potatoes, pearl onions. The gravy heavy and tasty. Jackson hadn't realized how hungry he was.

"So, why was she arrested?"

"It's complicated," says Jill. "I'm not sure I understand all of it."

Jackson puts his fork to one side. "Have you talked to Darlene?"

"Briefly. She was crying."

"And?"

Jill shrugs. "She says it's not her fault."

"Because nothing ever is," says Jackson.

"Jackson . . ."

"Okay, okay."

"She wasn't making much sense," says Jill. "I told the police that you would go down and deal with the situation."

"Me?"

"You're better at stuff like this than I am." Jill wipes Button's mouth. "Besides, I have to look after you-know-who."

"Me?" says Button.

"Yes, you little monkey."

"Not a monkey."

"How about we let her deal with the mess herself?" says Jackson. "She might learn something."

Jill clears the dishes. "There's cherry pie when you get back."

JACKSON MEETS WITH TWO police officers. Constable Virone and Constable Souto.

"Jackson Mosley."

"And you're the father?"

"Stepfather," says Jackson. "What did Darlene do?"

"Do you know a Mrs. Thea Karras?"

Jackson frowns. "Karras? Nico's mother?"

"That's right," says Souto. "Do you know the family?"

"Play golf with Nico. Don't know his mother."

"She's dead," says Virone. "That's part of the problem."

JACKSON IS ABLE TO get Darlene released into his custody. On the way home, she leans against the passenger side door, doesn't say anything.

"I don't see why I can't stay at the house."

"The house you broke into?"

"I didn't break in," says Darlene. "Mrs. Karras asked me to stay. Said I was like a daughter to her."

"She's dead."

"Not my fault," says Darlene. "Why do you always blame me for everything?"

"And then you stole things from the house?"

Darlene explodes. "I didn't steal anything. I borrowed some stuff. Mrs. Karras said I could."

"The dead woman."

"She was just dead at the end," says Darlene. "And all the stuff I borrowed, I brought back."

Jackson pulls the car into the driveway, turns off the engine.

"Except for the TV dinners that Billy ate."

"Billy? . . . Why can't I stay at Mrs. Karras's place?"

"Because it's not yours."

"I could look after it."

"Like you look after my place?"

"No one understands how hard my life is."

Darlene opens the door, gets out, slams the door shut as hard as she can. Jackson watches her hurry down the street, her shoulders hunched up around her neck, her arms holding her body together.

JILL IS IN THE living room, watching an *Elementary* rerun.

"Pie?"

Jill doesn't move from the sofa. "In the refrigerator."

Jackson puts the slice of pie on a plate, takes it to the table.

"Sherlock has relapsed," Jill tells him.

"Button in bed?"

"He is." The program goes to commercial. Jill stays on the sofa. "So, tell me."

"You remember Nico Karras's mother?"

"Vaguely."

"Thea. Older woman. Used to have a house on Manzanita. Nico got her a place at Autumn Leaves."

"The retirement home."

"Was trying to sell the house. Chuck Mason has the listing."

Jill makes a face. "That's the guy who won't pay you."

"The same." Jackson takes a forkful of pie. "Anyway, seems Mrs. Karras ran away from the retirement place and wound up back in her old house."

"Swallows to Capistrano."

"According to the police, Darlene found Mrs. Karras's purse in a bathroom at the hospital and returned it to her."

"That was nice."

"Without any money," says Jackson. "If I'm guessing."

"That's mean, Jackson."

"She used to steal money from your purse. So, she knows where to look."

"That was when she was younger. Did the police say she stole money?"

Jackson has another forkful. "Sometime after Darlene returned the purse, Mrs. Karras was found dead."

Jill mutes the sound on the TV. "Do they think that Darlene . . ."

"No," says Jackson. "The old lady died of natural causes, but it looks as though Darlene took a number of items from the house and then brought them back."

Jill waits.

"Yeah, it doesn't make a lot of sense. Darlene's story is that she returned the purse and that Mrs. Karras gave her a toaster and a lamp as a reward for being honest, and that the old lady was alive when she left the house."

"A toaster and a lamp?"

"And then when she heard that Mrs. Karras had died, Darlene felt bad about taking the toaster and the lamp and brought them back."

"Okay."

"Which is when the police caught her."

"Are they going to charge her?"

"Yet to be determined," says Jackson. "They released her on OR."

"Where is she?"

Jackson finished the pie, thinks about having a second piece.

"No idea. She told me that I blame her for everything."

Jill gets off the sofa, comes to the table, sits next to Jackson. "You didn't sign up for this."

Jackson pushes the plate to one side.

"And I don't think it's going to get better." Jill puts a hand on Jackson's arm. "I'm guessing we're going to have to raise Jor-El."

"Button."

"Can't turn my back on my daughter. Or my grandson."

Jackson looks out the window. Evening has come and gone.

"So, I need to know if you're up for this."

"Why do you think the aliens landed on the moon?"

"What?"

"I mean, there are nicer places to land. Florida, for instance. Or New Zealand. Or the French Riviera."

"Jackson," Jill whispers. "In or out?"

The NEXT MORNING, JACKSON goes to his old house. He expects to find Darlene there, but the place is empty. Except for Zoltan, the slobber hound who has evidently been stuck in the house for days with little to eat or drink. There are several piles of dog shit in the living room and signs there the dog has peed on the furniture.

"Fuck."

Zoltan slinks into a corner, turns around a couple of times, and then falls down in a heap.

"Fuck, fuck, fuck."

Jackson stands in the middle of the living room and waits until his mind and body come back to life.

Then he goes to work.

He cleans up the mess the dog has made, sprays deodorizer on the carpet and the furniture. Then he goes from room to room, picking up clothes and putting them in black plastic bags. He sets Button's clothes and toys to one side and saves some of Darlene's better outfits.

The rest of the bags he throws into the back of his pickup.

AT THE SHELTER, HE explains to the woman at the desk that his daughter has just taken a job in Red Deer, and that she can't take her dog with her.

"You can ship a dog by air," the woman at the desk tells him.

"Place she has in Red Deer doesn't allow pets."

"What's the dog's name?"

"Zoltan."

When Jackson says the name, the dog leans into his leg.

The woman smiles. "He seems to like you. Have you considered adopting him?"

"Not a pet person."

"There's a fee for leaving a pet with us."

Jackson rubs his face. "Of course there is."

LATER THAT AFTERNOON, JACKSON changes the cylinders on all the doors of his house and begins cleaning the place top to bottom. It will take several days, and the smell of dog shit will linger awhile.

But with any luck, by the end of the week, he'll be able to move back in.

erb has no idea how long he has sat on the bench in the Calgary airport. He's gotten up several times. Once to get a sandwich and a bottle of water. Twice to go to the bathroom. Once to go to the airline desk to ask about flights to Toronto.

And to Lethbridge.

Toronto. Lethbridge. Those are the choices.

His first inclination is to get on a plane and go home, back to his drive-in. He doesn't necessarily miss the place. Doesn't miss the movies or hitting golf balls at the screen, or the Launch Pad with its double bed and recliner.

His second inclination is to catch a flight to Lethbridge, check into that hotel on the edge of the coulees, and call Leroy. Going to Sun Dance might help him clear his head, take away some of the ache of having outlived Katherine, and the twins.

But it's been a long time since he's been back. He'll be a stranger in a strange land, his place within the community forfeited long ago. Still, Leroy would be happy to see him. That might be enough.

And then back to his bench. That's how he imagines it. His bench. At one point, a woman in a vest and a cowboy hat comes.

"I've noticed you sitting there," says the woman. "Are you okay?"

The woman has a sheriff's badge on her vest that says INFORMATION.

"Fine," Herb tells her.

"Nothing wrong with sitting in the airport," says the woman. "It's just odd."

"I wanted to rent a car," says Herb, trying to be friendly, "but they're all sold out."

"Stampede," says the woman. "Name's Coreen. Coreen with a *C*. This is my job. Help people get from the airport to the Stampede grounds. Help them with hotels and such."

"Busy."

"That's why the car rental places are all sold out." Coreen gives Herb a wink. "Like this every year. Thought they might cancel it 'cause of the aliens, but then the little green buggers skedaddled."

"The aliens left?"

"Hell's bells," says the woman, "don't you watch TV?"

"Not much."

"Aliens were smart enough to see that we're no one they want to mess with. Truth be told, we scare the sugar out of ourselves."

"Think I'm heading to Lethbridge."

"Lethbridge?" says the woman. "You must like wind."

Herb has forgotten about the chinooks that slide off the eastern face of the Rockies and flatten everything in their path. How could he have forgotten the wind?

And Chief Mountain.

What was it that the people used to say? If you could see the mountain, you knew you were home.

"It blows pretty good."

"About the only good way to get there is to fly in," says the woman. "You know how to get to the domestic terminal?"

"But I may just go back to Toronto."

The woman makes a face. "Not a place I want to visit."

Herb thanks the woman for her consideration, heads to the bathroom for his third visit. Then he comes back to the bench and sits down.

HERB DOESN'T SEE THE Stampede woman again. Evening turns into night, night turns into morning, morning to afternoon. He wonders if there is a statute of limitations on sitting in an airport, figures that it's like a mall, where people come and go but don't stay.

If the police show up, he'll tell them that he's waiting for an omen, a sign of some sort. If they press him, he'll flip a coin.

The blond woman sitting on a bench on the other side of the concourse looks familiar. Blond, thin, with one bag that she holds on her lap. Karen, no, Ellen. Ellen Tidy. At least, the woman looks like Ellen Tidy. He's met Gary Tidy's wife before, when Katherine was alive, when he played golf at the club.

A lifetime ago.

But it might not be Ellen. She could be a complete stranger, and Herb doesn't want to stare. He could get up, walk over, introduce himself. If she's not Ellen, he'd apologize, no harm done. If it is Ellen, he could say hello, maybe invite her to have coffee while he waits for his omen to come along.

Maybe the woman on the bench is that omen.

Herb stands up. He's stiff from sitting. He takes several steps forward, then stops. What is he thinking? It doesn't matter whether the woman is Ellen Tidy or not. What is to be gained by talking to her? How will hearing her voice help with the decision at hand?

Go. Stay. Stay. Go.

Herb turns, wanders down the concourse, stops at Virgin Books, browses about in the Heritage Trading Post, contemplates a beverage at Jugo Juice.

And when he gets back to his bench, the woman is gone.

XXVI

Darby Dock is at her desk at Autumn Leaves. She's on the phone with the real estate agent in Victoria.

"What do you mean you can't get in?"

As if she didn't have enough trouble. First, Mrs. Karras, and now this.

"What do you mean he's not there?"

XXVII

The *Splendour of the Seas* is better than he could have possibly imagined. Richard, Dick to his family, sees clearly now that Ed is wrong about cruises, and Dick suspects that Ed is simply envious of people, such as himself, who are able to sail away into the world.

From the moment the steward opened the door to his stateroom, Dick knew that this is what he had been working toward all his life. Yes, it's smaller than his condo in Victoria. But not by much. And elegant, with a sliding glass door and a balcony, where he can sit and watch the ocean pass beneath the ship.

He spends a whole day walking through all the amenities. Several pools, all with elaborate waterslides, one with a wave machine for body surfing. A go-kart track. A driving range and putting green. Skeet shooting. A rock-climbing wall. A theatre. Floor shows every night. A casino. An art gallery.

And the food. My god, the food is incredible. Everywhere Dick looks there are restaurants upon restaurants, food, food, food, for the taking. And if he's exhausted from all the activities, he can ring for room service.

Dick wishes that Darby could see him now. He'll send her a postcard from their first port of call.

In the meantime, he has to get dressed. There is a meet and greet for singles in the jazz bar. Dick is glad he remembered to bring his business cards with him.

Richard Dock. Editor-in-chief of *Camosack: Victoria's Lifestyle Magazine*.

Who needs MillionaireMatch or Ashley Madison? He has an entire shipload of possibilities. And he doesn't have to fill out a stupid questionnaire.

Dick runs a hand through his hair. He's looking particularly debonair. He might even say dashing and, yes, desirable. And no longer needing to be invisible.

He's reminded of a large poster in the main lounge. A photograph of a young couple with champagne glasses. The man's shirt is open, revealing a hard stomach. The woman is in a skimpy bikini. Dick had paused in front of the image.

That could be him.

That is him.

Dick smiles at his reflection in the mirror. Checks his teeth for any signs of the excellent prime rib dinner, squirts some of the cologne that comes free with the room into the air.

And steps into the mist.